The Desert Flowers –
Mistletoe and Holly – 4

Judith Keim

BOOKS BY JUDITH KEIM

SEASHELL COTTAGE BOOKS:

A Christmas Star
Change of Heart
A Summer of Surprises
A Road Trip to Remember
The Beach Babes

THE DESERT SAGE INN SERIES:

The Desert Flowers – Rose – 1
The Desert Flowers – Lily – 2
The Desert Flowers – Willow – 3
The Desert Flowers – Mistletoe & Holly – 4

SOUL SISTERS AT CEDAR MOUNTAIN LODGE:

Christmas Sisters – Anthology
Christmas Kisses
Christmas Castles
Christmas Stories – Soul Sisters Anthology
Christmas Joy

THE SANDERLING COVE INN SERIES:

Waves of Hope
Sandy Wishes – (2023)
Salty Kisses – (2023)

THE LILAC LAKE INN SERIES

Love by Design – (2023)
Love Between the Lines – (2023)
Love Under the Stars – (2024)

OTHER BOOKS:

The ABC's of Living With a Dachshund
Once Upon a Friendship – Anthology
Winning BIG – a little love story for all ages
Holiday Hopes
The Winning Tickets – (2023)

PRAISE FOR JUDITH KEIM'S NOVELS

THE BEACH HOUSE HOTEL SERIES

"Love the characters in this series. This series was my first introduction to Judith Keim. She is now one of my favorites. Looking forward to reading more of her books."

BREAKFAST AT THE BEACH HOUSE HOTEL is an easy, delightful read that offers romance, family relationships, and strong women learning to be stronger. Real life situations filter through the pages. Enjoy!"

LUNCH AT THE BEACH HOUSE HOTEL – "This series is such a joy to read. You feel you are actually living with them. Can't wait to read the latest one."

DINNER AT THE BEACH HOUSE HOTEL – "A Terrific Read! As usual, Judith Keim did it again. Enjoyed immensely. Continue writing such pleasantly reading books for all of us readers."

CHRISTMAS AT THE BEACH HOUSE HOTEL – "Not Just Another Christmas Novel. This is book number four in the series and my introduction to Judith Keim's writing. I wasn't disappointed. The characters are dimensional and engaging. The plot is well crafted and advances at a pleasing pace. The Florida location is interesting and warming. It was a delight to read a romance novel with mature female protagonists. Ann and Rhoda have life experiences that enrich the story. It's a clever book about friends and extended family. Buy copies for your book group and enjoy this seasonal read."

MARGARITAS AT THE BEACH HOUSE HOTEL – "What a wonderful series. I absolutely loved this book and can't wait for the next book to come out. There was even suspense in it. Thanks Judith for the great stories."

"Overall, *Margaritas at the Beach House Hotel* is another wonderful addition to the series. Judith Keim takes the reader on a journey told through the voices of these amazing characters we have all come to love through the years! I truly cannot stress enough how good this book is, and I hope you enjoy it as much as I have!"

THE HARTWELL WOMEN SERIES:

"This was an EXCELLENT series. When I discovered Judith Keim, I read all of her books back to back. I thoroughly enjoyed the women Keim has written about. They are believable and you want to just jump into their lives and be their friends! I can't wait for any upcoming books!"

"I fell into Judith Keim's Hartwell Women series and have read & enjoyed all of her books in every series. Each centers around a strong & interesting woman character and their family interaction. Good reads that leave you wanting more."

THE FAT FRIDAYS GROUP :

"Excellent story line for each character, and an insightful representation of situations which deal with some of the contemporary issues women are faced with today."

"I love this author's books. Her characters and their lives are realistic. The power of women's friendships is a common and beautiful theme that is threaded throughout this story."

THE SALTY KEY INN SERIES

FINDING ME – "I thoroughly enjoyed the first book in this series and cannot wait for the others! The characters are endearing with the same struggles we all encounter. The setting makes me feel like I am a guest at The Salty Key Inn...relaxed, happy & light-hearted! The men are yummy and the women strong. You can't get better than that!

FINDING MY WAY- *"Loved the family dynamics as well as uncertain emotions of dating and falling in love. Appreciated the morals and strength of parenting throughout. Just couldn't put this book down."*

FINDING LOVE – *"I waited for this book because the first two was such good reads. This one didn't disappoint.... Judith Keim always puts substance into her books. This book was no different, I learned about PTSD, accepting oneself, there is always going to be problems but stick it out and make it work. Just the way life is. In some ways a lot like my life. Judith is right, it needs another book and I will definitely be reading it. Hope you choose to read this series.*

FINDING FAMILY – *"Completing this series is like eating the last chip. Love Judith's writing, and her female characters are always smart, strong, vulnerable to life and love experiences."*

"This was a refreshing book. Bringing the heart and soul of the family to us."

THE CHANDLER HILL INN SERIES

GOING HOME – *"I absolutely could not put this book down. Started at night and read late into the middle of the night. As a child of the '60s, the Vietnam war was front and center so this resonated with me. All the characters in the book were so well developed that the reader felt like they were friends of the family."*

"I was completely immersed in this book, with the beautiful descriptive writing, and the authors' way of bringing her characters to life. I felt like I was right inside her story."

COMING HOME – *"Coming Home is a winner. The characters are well-developed, nuanced and likable. Enjoyed* the vineyard setting, learning about wine growing and seeing the challenges Cami faces in running and growing a business. I look forward to the next book in this series!"

"Coming Home was such a wonderful story. The author has a gift for getting the reader right to the heart of things."

HOME AT LAST – "In this wonderful conclusion, to a heartfelt and emotional trilogy set in Oregon's stunning wine country, Judith Keim has tied up the Chandler Hill series with the perfect bow."

"Overall, this is truly a wonderful addition to the Chandler Hill Inn series. Judith Keim definitely knows how to perfectly weave together a beautiful and heartfelt story."

"The storyline has some beautiful scenes along with family drama. Judith Keim has created characters with interactions that are believable and some of the subjects the story deals with are poignant."

SEASHELL COTTAGE BOOKS

A CHRISTMAS STAR – "Love, laughter, sadness, great food, and hope for the future, all in one book. It doesn't get any better than this stunning read."

"A Christmas Star is a heartwarming Christmas story featuring endearing characters. So many Christmas books are set in snowbound places...it was a nice change to read a Christmas story that takes place on a warm sandy beach!" Susan Peterson

CHANGE OF HEART – "CHANGE OF HEART is the summer read we've all been waiting for. Judith Keim is a master at creating fascinating characters that are simply irresistible. Her stories leave you with a big smile on your face and a heart bursting with love."

Kellie Coates Gilbert, author of the popular Sun Valley Series

A SUMMER OF SURPRISES – *"The story is filled with a roller coaster of emotions and self-discovery. Finding love again and rebuilding family relationships."*

"Ms. Keim uses this book as an amazing platform to show that with hard emotional work, belief in yourself and love, the scars of abuse can be conquered. It in no way preaches, it's a lovely story with a happy ending."

"The character development was excellent. I felt I knew these people my whole life. The story development was very well thought out I was drawn [in] from the beginning."

THE DESERT SAGE INN SERIES:

THE DESERT FLOWERS – ROSE – *"The Desert Flowers - Rose, is the first book in the new series by Judith Keim. I always look forward to new books by Judith Keim, and this one is definitely a wonderful way to begin The Desert Sage Inn Series!"*

"In this first of a series, we see each woman come into her own and view new beginnings even as they must take this tearful journey as they slowly lose a dear friend. This is a very well written book with well-developed and likable main characters. It was interesting and enlightening as the first portion of this saga unfolded. I very much enjoyed this book and I do recommend it"

"Judith Keim is one of those authors that you can always depend on to give you a great story with fantastic characters. I'm excited to know that she is writing a new series and after reading book 1 in the series, I can't wait to read the rest of the books."!

THE DESERT FLOWERS – LILY – *"The second book in the Desert Flowers series is just as wonderful as the first.*

Judith Keim is a brilliant storyteller. Her characters are truly lovely and people that you want to be friends with as soon as you start reading. Judith Keim is not afraid to weave real life conflict and loss into her stories. I loved reading Lily's story and can't wait for Willow's!

"The Desert Flowers Lily is the second book in The Desert Sage Inn Series by author Judith Keim. When I read the first book in the series, The Desert Flowers-Rose, I knew this series would exceed all of my expectations and then some. Judith Keim is an amazing author, and this series is a testament to her writing skills and her ability to completely draw a reader into the world of her characters."

THE DESERT FLOWERS – WILLOW – "The feelings of love, joy, happiness, friendship, family and the pain of loss are deeply felt by Willow Sanchez and her two cohorts Rose and Lily. The Desert Flowers met because of their deep feelings for Alec Thurston, a man who touched their lives in different ways."

"Once again, Judith Keim has written the story of a strong, competent, confident and independent woman. Willow, like Rose and Lily can handle tough situations. All the characters are written so that the reader gets to know them but not all the characters will give the reader warm and fuzzy feelings."

"The story is well written and from the start you will be pulled in. There is enough backstory that a reader can start here but I assure you, you'll want to learn more. There is an ocean of emotions that will make you smile, cringe, tear up or out right cry. I loved this book as I loved books one and two. I am thrilled that the Desert Flowers story will continue. I highly recommend this book to anyone who enjoys books with strong women."

The Desert Flowers – Mistletoe and Holly

A Desert Sage Inn Book - 4

Judith Keim

Wild Quail Publishing

wildquail.pub@gmail.com
www.judithkeim.com

Wild Quail Publishing
PO Box 171332
Boise, ID 83717-1332

ISBN 978-1-954325-34-0

Dedication

For all my loyal readers

CHAPTER ONE
JUANITA

On this bright, blue-sky day in October, Juanita Sanchez climbed out of her car in Palm Desert, California and went to greet the three women whom her family friend and former employer, Alec Thurston, had named the Desert Flowers—her daughter, Willow, Rose Macklin Bowers, and Lily Weaver Walden. They were standing in front of a building Lily was suggesting for their special, newly-formed Juanita's Kitchen project.

Upon Alec's death, Juanita and the Desert Flowers women decided to open a charity with a portion of the bequests Alec had left them. To Juanita's delight, all three of the young women had insisted the charity be named for her for the help she'd faithfully given to Alec for years.

As she walked toward them, Juanita thought the three Flowers were as pretty as their names. Smart too. As Alec was dying of cancer, he'd requested each of them to come to California to use their business skills to help him with the ownership transition of his resort, the Desert Sage Inn, to The Blaise Hotel Group. No one had hesitated. Alec was beloved by each of them for different reasons.

"Juanita, glad you're here. We think this might be the right one," said Rose, waving her over. The oldest of the Flowers at fifty-two, Rose was the tallest and most flamboyant with her red hair and green eyes.

"I hope you like it," said petite, blonde Lily. "We've pretty much run out of places to look at if we want to get the food kitchen up and running before the holidays."

"I'll know if this feels right," said Juanita. For her it was as much a spiritual choice as a practical one. She stared at the sturdy, two-story, brown-stucco building they were thinking of purchasing. It sat on a side street in the middle of the downtown area. Twice, they'd thought they'd found the right place, had even received the mayor's approval for one of them, and then backed out after an owner decided not to sell in one case and after pre-sale inspections were made in another.

Her daughter, Willow, a dark-haired beauty about to get married, looped an arm around her. "We're pretty excited about this one, but if you feel the building isn't right, we won't go ahead with it."

Juanita smiled at her. "If it's right, I'll feel Alec's approval." If he hadn't been generous to all of them, they wouldn't be able to move forward with this charitable idea—something they knew would please him.

Juanita studied the exterior of the building. It was in fairly good shape. It would require just a little dressing up, a fresh coat of paint on the stucco and on the wooden window trim, maybe in a nice beige with turquoise trim. Attention to the parking lot, repainting parking lines, and planting additional landscaping would make a big difference, and could easily be done. Her husband, Pedro, had worked for Alec as a landscaper for years while she worked in his kitchen and managed the house for him. Pedro would make the plantings look really nice.

Rose walked to the front door, opened it, and held it for her as Juanita made her way inside, eager to see the possibilities there.

"I know it's a mess," said Lily behind her, "but I believe the bones of the building are good."

Juanita faced a large main room with windows on both

sides that would let in sunlight and give it a nice atmosphere. From there, Lily led her down a hallway into the back where a kitchen filled with grubby pans and dirty countertops displayed evidence of a previous owner's activities.

"We'll have someone look at expanding the kitchen and tearing down some of the walls alongside it," said Rose. "But storage rooms will remain."

"Upstairs, like we talked about for the other places, we'll put an office and a couple of ensuite bedrooms in case staff members need to stay there from time to time," said Willow.

Lily gave her a hopeful smile. "I really think this one can work, Juanita."

Juanita nodded and walked back to the open front door. Turning and facing inside, she stood in a ray of sunshine that entered the building in a lemony wash of warmth. Closing her eyes, she let the image of what the Flowers described take shape in her mind. She imagined she could hear the sounds of people working in the kitchen, others coming through the door to get a hot, noonday meal they couldn't afford otherwise. More than that, she felt Alec's approval.

She opened her eyes and smiled. "This has a good feeling. Let's take a closer look around."

"Wonderful!" cried Lily, her brown eyes alight with excitement.

"I've already called an inspection company," said Rose. "They'll meet with us this afternoon, if it's agreeable with everyone. We have a short-term option on the building to protect our interests, but we still have to move quickly to get ready for the holidays."

Juanita laughed. It was so like Rose to be ahead of everyone else. "Okay, let's do it."

###

A couple of months later, Juanita walked into the large front room they were using as a dining room and gazed at the fresh, cream-colored paint on the walls. Behind it, workmen were busily putting in both new and second-hand kitchen appliances, and others were working on building out the service area. The sound of their work was magical. What had started as a dream was coming to fruition.

Interviews for the six-member staff were taking place in a private office at Juanita's church. Several of the candidates had been referred from that source. Their plan was to offer work to those who might not easily find work elsewhere.

Filled with excitement, Juanita left the building and hurried over to the church. Rose would meet her there. Together they hoped to recommend candidates to Willow and Lily. Then, they'd all decide what they could do to help those individuals.

Outside the office, waiting for an interview, a number of people were sitting in chairs lined up against the wall, including a young woman with a boy.

Rose met her at the door to the private office. "A lot of people have shown up. It looks like we might have a good selection."

"Great." Juanita was counting on Rose to be her usual sensible self because Juanita knew she'd want to hire them all. She set down her purse, sat behind the desk, and looked through the notes Rose had made—reminders to ask specific questions.

Rose opened the door and called out the name of the first person.

Seated in one of the two chairs facing them, the woman answered their questions, fidgeting nervously. Juanita knew how tough it was for some people to tell their stories.

One face became two, then three, then four. A blur of unhappy circumstances, rays of hope.

The young woman she'd seen with a boy came into the office with him in tow. Juanita studied his sweet face, his shining eyes. When he looked right at her and grinned, her heart filled.

They quickly learned his mother, Ivy Barrett, was in her early twenties, and her son, Benjy, was seven. She'd left her home in the South with him at eighteen and had worked in resorts since that time. Now she was studying for her Associates Degree in the Culinary Management program at the College of the Desert.

As they chatted, Juanita understood that Ivy's background was a painful one. When questioned, Ivy made it plain she had no plans ever to return to the South, that her family didn't want them. She also said they were living in temporary quarters in an apartment that wasn't in a good area and she was looking for something better for her son. She explained she had no babysitter which is why she'd brought her child to the interview.

Juanita kept darting looks at him. During this conversation, Benjy sat with a book, leafing through the pages as if he'd heard this conversation before.

Juanita and Rose probed for more information about Ivy's ability to handle pressure in a kitchen, oversee staff, and what her thoughts were about the idea behind Juanita's Kitchen.

"I think it's a wonderful program, a much-needed one. From a staffer's point of view, I see no difference between feeding someone in a high-end resort and a crowd in Juanita's Kitchen. I know what it's like to be on the receiving end."

Rose and Juanita exchanged glances of approval.

"We'd very much like you to meet our other two partners.

Are you available tomorrow?"

Ivy nodded. "Yes, I'd like that a lot. Thank you."

"And feel free to bring Benjy. He's been so good," said Juanita smiling at him.

After phone numbers were exchanged and times agreed upon, Ivy stood. "Come, Benjy. Time to go."

Benjy gave them a little wave. "See y'all tomorrow."

Juanita chuckled. Such a bright little boy. He hadn't missed a word of their conversation.

The next day, Juanita and Rose presented their choice of six candidates to Willow and Lily, and the four of them all agreed they were perfect. Only one man, Isaac Newman, was selected to be part of the staff. The rest were women of varying ages.

As another part of their plan, Juanita and the Flowers spent considerable time to help get three of the women into apartments of their own. Only two didn't require that kind of assistance. Isaac lived with his sister, and Summer Hunter lived with her boyfriend. It was decided that Ivy and Benjy would live in the rooms above the kitchen, and in exchange for keeping watch over the property, Ivy would be given a small bonus.

With growing anticipation, the days crept closer to the grand opening.

CHAPTER TWO
JUANITA

*I*t's really going to happen!" Juanita Sanchez thought, clasping her hands thankfully. On this early-December day, she gathered with the three Desert Flowers in front of Juanita's Kitchen. A sign next to the front door proudly declared the name, "Juanita's Kitchen", and a welcome to all to enter.

"I'm so excited about this. It's perfect," said Lily, letting out a happy sigh.

Juanita stared at the building they'd purchased and converted for its new purpose. It had been worth the wait to find it. But they'd all had to work hard as it became a race against time to open it before the holidays.

Inside, they'd reconfigured the floor layout by relocating some walls to create an even larger space on the first floor to serve as a dining room. The kitchen behind the dining room had been enlarged and equipped with the best of second-hand or new appliances, including a professional, commercial gas range that would make any chef proud, and a rack-style commercial dishwasher installed next to a double stainless steel sink intended for pot washing. A second-hand, two-section reach-in refrigerator/freezer had been located adjacent to the back entrance to the kitchen to accommodate easy deliveries and storage of refrigerated and frozen products. Perimeter shelving around the kitchen provided easily accessible storage for dry goods.

Upstairs, a sizeable office had been set up to run Juanita's

Kitchen, along with two bedrooms and full baths that Ivy and Benjy were occupying.

"Juanita's Kitchen has a nice ring to it, doesn't it," said Willow, placing an arm around her. "I'm proud of you, Mom."

"Thanks, *Cariña.*" Juanita was still flattered that the women had chosen her name for the charity. She'd enjoyed cooking for Alec for years, while her husband, Pedro, did other work for him. Now, instead of cooking for family and friends, she would oversee a staff who'd cook a hot meal for those who couldn't afford it on their own. A life circle, one might say, because as a young girl growing up in Mexico, she'd helped her mother do the same for others in their small hometown.

Juanita's thoughts flew to the past. She and Pedro might never have come to Palm Desert if her cousin, Conchita, hadn't traveled to the Desert Sage Inn to work at Alec's hotel. Conchita and Alec quickly fell in love and married. But tragedy struck a crushing blow when Conchita became trapped in a house fire that she and their unborn baby girl didn't survive.

After learning what had happened and discovering how devastated Alec was, Juanita knew she had to step in and help him, in honor of the cousin she'd loved like a sister. She'd talked it over with Pedro, and they came to help Alec through his grief, bringing Willow, their young daughter, with them.

Alec never stopped blaming himself for not being there to save his family. At first, only Willow's sweet and curious nature could draw Alec from the depths of his depression. Slowly, he was able to carry on and set to work expanding his hotel, building it into the outstanding resort it was today. His recent death from cancer was not the terrible thing for him that it was for those he left behind. They all understood. He wanted to be with Conchita again.

Willow turned to her and smiled. "The grand opening

tomorrow is going to be great."

Juanita bobbed her head. "A long time coming, but a dream of mine. Alec would be so pleased to see how we've all worked together to make this happen."

"I love that you're carrying on your family practice of cooking for others in this way," Rose said warmly. "It's a beautiful tradition."

Lily gave Juanita a careful hug. At forty-two and with a baby due in just four weeks, she was overly cautious about doing anything to harm the baby. "Once someone tastes your food, we'll never have enough for everyone."

Juanita chuckled. It was true. People loved her cooking. She was thankful for this project. Working on it helped fill the hole she'd been feeling after losing Alec and the role she'd played in his house for so many years. And with Willow's upcoming marriage, she'd been feeling at loose ends.

As she went into the kitchen, Juanita smiled and nodded to the kitchen staff. The six of them were an unlikely crew, but she and the Flowers had seen something special in each of them.

Ivy waved in acknowledgement and went back to giving directions to the other five. Juanita and the Flowers hadn't hesitated to appoint Ivy their kitchen supervisor. She was bright, eager to learn, and talented in the kitchen.

Even now, Ivy was going over kitchen protocol one last time with the staff. The health codes regarding food storage, preparation, and service and other business requirements from both state and local officials for running the kitchen were onerous and required specific training and certification for the staff.

Benjy came into sight, saw Juanita, and came running over to her. "Nita! Nita!"

Juanita's heart burst with love as she hugged him to her.

They'd bonded from the first moment they'd met. It was as if he knew between Alec's death and Willow's upcoming marriage and making a home of her own, Juanita had an empty space inside her.

After a moment, Benjy wiggled to get free. She let him go and watched him run back to the little room off the kitchen. It was being used as a toy room for the children of some of the women on the crew.

Isaac noticed her and a wide smile crossed his face, creasing his chocolate-colored skin at the corners of his big brown eyes. Again, Juanita's heart filled. Isaac was a giant of a man, who was as gentle as could be, almost child-like, after suffering a brain injury serving in the military. At present, unable to work a normal, full-time job, he was living in the area with his sister. The minister at Juanita's church had recommended Isaac among others to her, and, after meeting him, she and all three Desert Flowers eagerly agreed to hire him.

"Is everyone set with their schedules?" Juanita asked. "Remember, if for any reason you must make a change to it, you need to get in touch with us immediately."

All heads nodded.

Ivy held up a sheet of paper. "Rose gave us each a list of phone numbers."

Staff members were required to be at the Juanita's Kitchen from 9 AM until 3 PM Monday through Saturday, less one day off, so the facility could open for meals at noon. On Sundays, it was expected that most of their guests would get meals that churches in the area provided. As the need grew, volunteers would help serve hot food and prepare sack lunches for guests to take home to enjoy later in the day.

Juanita left the kitchen and climbed the stairs to join the other Flowers in the office. At the top, she paused and checked

Benjy's room. It was surprisingly neat. But he and his mother were used to moving around, and he didn't have many possessions to worry about. The bonus of having Benjy around was something Juanita treasured. She loved that little boy, his sparkling light-brown eyes, the soft brown curls on his head.

His mother was as blonde as Benjy was brown and was as reserved a tough survivor as any young woman Juanita had ever known. Though Juanita and Ivy hadn't yet grown especially close, they had an understanding between them to allow Benjy his sweet relationship with her.

"Good morning," she called in a cheerful voice as she entered the office.

"Glad you're here," said Willow. "We're discussing Christmas decorations."

Later, after she and the Flowers finalized plans for Christmas decorations and agreed on resolutions for other issues, Juanita glanced at her watch and went downstairs to check on the crew's progress.

"How's everyone doing?" she asked, walking into the kitchen and placing a hand on Rosita Castello's shoulder. Rosita at thirty-three was the mother of three children—two girls aged fourteen and twelve, and a little boy of two. Her background was a tough one. Her long-time boyfriend had gotten into drugs and was now in prison for murder. The two-year-old boy, Paco, was the son of a man who'd been killed in the army. Rosita and he had never married.

"Ah think we've covered everything lak y'all asked," said Ivy.

"Time for me to get home," Rosita said. "I have just a short time to be with the kids and prepare for my night job." Juanita and the Flowers liked Rosita's determination to get back on her feet and show her daughters how to be strong.

"We'll see you all tomorrow morning promptly at nine. Be sure to wear the T-shirts we've given you. We want to look professional." Juanita turned to Ivy. "Anything you want to add?"

Ivy shook her head. "We'll be good. Right, all y'all?"

All heads bobbed.

"Okay, then. See you tomorrow," Juanita said.

Ivy approached her. "You don't mind if I leave early for my class?"

"No, I know you want to study for your exam, and I love having Benjy here with me."

Juanita took care of him in the afternoon three times a week while Ivy attended classes at the College of the Desert.

"Mama's going to school?" Benjy said. "Ah'm not!" He gave her an impish grin and took hold of her hand. "Let's play."

Juanita laughed, wishing life could stay like this for him forever.

The three Flowers came down the stairs.

"We're set with the decorations like we discussed," said Rose. "Hank and I will shop for them this afternoon. Want to come?"

Juanita shook her head. "Thanks, but I'm staying with Benjy until Ivy gets back from her class, and then Pedro and I are going out to dinner for a celebration of sorts before our opening tomorrow. But no worries. We'll help put up the decorations this evening."

"Sounds good," said Rose.

"I've got to get home to relieve Anna from babysitting and watch the kids myself," said Lily. "I'll see you later." Lily's story of how she and her husband Brian had unexpectedly ended up with a son and a daughter was both sad and sweet.

Juanita gave Lily a hug. "Remember, you shouldn't feel you have to spend the whole day here tomorrow. Not at your stage of pregnancy. We've got it covered."

"Thanks. I'll definitely be here when we open for our first meal," Lily said, giving them all a wave. "See you tomorrow for sure."

After she left, Rose said, "I'm going to pick up Hank now. It's a good time to tackle the shopping for decorations."

"Sorry Craig and I can't meet you for dinner tonight," Willow said to her. "More wedding plans. But we'll make it another night. I promise. Now, I've gotta go." She kissed Juanita goodbye. "See you later when we decorate. Eight o'clock. Right, Rose? Mom?"

Juanita and Rose nodded, and then Juanita stood at the doorway and bid everyone goodbye.

She looked down at Benjy. "Guess it's you and me."

Benjy nodded solemnly. "Yeah, Ah know."

Juanita hugged him to her wondering at the sad look that had crossed his face. There was a lot she still didn't know about Ivy and Benjy except the barest of details. Ivy had been, apparently, a wild child in her small Southern town and without parental love. At eighteen, discouraged, and with a two-year-old son, Ivy rejected the idea of staying anywhere close to her hometown. There, her strict, religious parents treated her like a harlot and refused to have anything to do with Benjy. After leaving home and working in one resort after another for five years, Ivy decided she liked the hospitality field enough to learn all she could about it and moved to Palm Desert.

"Before we play a game, let's have some juice and a cookie," Juanita said to Benjy. "Sound good?"

Benjy smiled, and then mimicking his mother's southern drawl, he replied, "Lak music to my e-uhs."

Juanita laughed, charmed as always by him.

CHAPTER THREE
JUANITA

Juanita poured a glass of apple juice for Benjy, set a homemade chocolate chip cookie on a napkin, and sat with him at the table they'd tucked into the corner of the kitchen. "Would you rather play a game or read a book?" Juanita asked him.

"Read a book about Nate," said Benjy, his eyes alight.

"Another adventure," said Juanita. Benjy was a bright boy. She loved the chance to cuddle on the couch and read to him. Sometimes they took turns reading aloud if the words weren't too difficult.

Later, they were on the couch together reading when Ivy appeared.

"How'd your class go?" Juanita said, giving her an encouraging smile.

"Okay. Ah know a lot of the stuff already, but Ah want that certificate and degree to make me more professional."

"Your resumé was very impressive," Juanita said quietly. She knew from past experience if she sounded too positive, Ivy wouldn't trust her kindness. Just one result of being treated poorly at home.

Ivy shrugged. "Thanks."

"You and I are going to make a wonderful team going forward," Juanita told her. "It's important because I need to rely on you when I'm not here. I know you can do it."

Ivy nodded and a slow smile crossed her young, pretty face. Of average height and trim, she was a lovely woman, not gorgeous, but attractive with blue eyes, clear skin, and a gentleness that appeared only when she was with her son. Though she was technically their boss, Ivy showed the other kitchen staff members respect, even when things didn't go right. That kindness meant a lot to Juanita, especially after knowing Ivy hadn't received it.

"We're coming back here tonight. You know about the decorating party tonight, right?" Juanita said.

Ivy nodded. "Yes, Benjy and I will stay out of your way."

"No, by all means, join us. We want you to share in the excitement. It's always such a fun time of year. I know Benjy will love it."

Ivy paused and then blurted, "Christmas isn't a fun time of year. Not for people like me. All Ah have are bad memories of the holidays." She shook her head and let out a sound of disgust. "Santa Claus and all. What a joke."

"Oh, Ivy," said Juanita, clamping a hand over her heart. "That makes me so sad."

"Sorry, but Ah learned early on no Santa Claus was comin' to mah house. Not then, not now."

"Well, what about Benjy here? Surely, he'd like to be part of decorating the place."

Ivy frowned and turned to him. "Benjy, you can help the ladies decorate, but don't you get any ideas 'bout Santa."

Benjy bit his lip and nodded. "Okay, Mama."

Juanita held back the words that wanted to spring from her throat. She couldn't interfere, but somehow, she'd have to convince them both that Santa Claus and the spirit of giving were alive and well.

She got to her feet. "Pedro and I are going out for pizza. Care to join us?"

Ivy shook her head. "Thanks, anyway, but I've got some homework Ah have to do." Her face brightened. "If you have any leftovers that sure would be nice."

"Deal," said Juanita, pleased to be able to do something for her. She checked her watch and called Pedro. "Meet me at Victor's. I'll be there shortly."

As soon as she walked into the small, crowded restaurant, the spicy aroma of tomato, garlic, and olive oil hit her nose with a teasing caress. She spied Pedro sitting in a booth toward the back and went over to him.

He rose and gave her a quick kiss. "Ordered a glass of wine for you."

"Thanks. As usual, it smells delicious in here. What are you having?"

"A couple of beers and my usual, sausage and pepperoni."

"I'm going to have a plain cheese pizza because I promised Ivy and Benjy leftovers and I'm not sure what they like best."

"How're they doing?" Pedro asked. "I told Benjy I'd let him help make a couple of things with me."

"What things?" Juanita said, shrugging out of her coat, sitting, and facing him across the table.

He grinned. "A few Christmas surprises."

She leaned closer. "Ivy doesn't believe in Santa Claus and doesn't want Benjy to think Santa's going to come to them." She shook her head. "It's a season for sharing and doing nice things for others whether you believe in Santa Claus or not. But the way Ivy was talking, she wanted none of that."

"Hmmm. Maybe if he helps me, Benjy will see things a little differently. Especially if one of the gifts is for his mother."

Juanita smiled, reached across the table, and gave Pedro's hand a loving squeeze. "Thank you, *mi amor.*"

Pedro grinned. "I see this little boy has found a way into your heart."

"Oh, yes, he certainly has," said Juanita. She sighed. "It feels good to have a little one around, someone to fill an empty part of me."

Pedro frowned. "Are you okay? You don't sound like yourself."

Juanita waved away his concern. "I'm just feeling a bit ... at odds ... with all the changes. Alec dying and my job disappearing makes things so different." She wondered if in her mid-fifties, menopause was taking another dig at her, making her feel so blue, so unneeded.

"Well, no time to worry about it," said Pedro. "Juanita's Kitchen opens tomorrow. Think how happy that would make Alec."

Juanita's lips curved. "It's a dream come true. For all of us."

They placed their orders for pizza and salad, and while they waited, they continued to share the day's events. They'd always been compatible. It was this ease between them that had helped Alec after Conchita's death, had encouraged him to become a real part of their small family.

When their pizza came, they quietly ate. Dining out, even for just pizza, was a treat. Something Juanita was enjoying more and more as her work grew at the Kitchen. And now that Pedro was semi-retired, he liked getting out and seeing people. He'd thought about applying for work at the Premio Inn, where Willow was the manager, but she'd gently told him she didn't think it was a good idea. He was still trying to decide whether to try to get a job elsewhere. Alec had left them enough money that it wasn't urgent.

When they entered Juanita's Kitchen, Hank and Rose were already there, standing in the middle of the dining room surrounded by bags and boxes.

"Look, Nita! It's decorations," said Benjy, his eyes alight with excitement. Then he caught sight of the pizza boxes. "Pizza? For me?"

Juanita laughed. "Yes, for you and your mama."

Ivy appeared at the top of the stairway. "Ah'll be down in a minute. Ah'm just finishin' up."

Juanita headed for the kitchen. Benjy pranced at her heels like a puppy. Ivy was very good about seeing that Benjy ate well, but he seemed to be in a growth spurt and was always hungry.

After getting him seated at the table, Juanita handed him a slice of pizza on a paper plate. She turned as Ivy walked into the kitchen to join them.

"Get all your homework done?" Juanita asked.

Ivy smiled and nodded. "For tonight. And a little bit for another class."

"Sounds good," said Juanita. "Have some pizza. I'm going to join the others in the dining room."

As Juanita walked into the main room, Willow and her fiancé, Craig, came through the doorway and joined them. Juanita hugged them both.

Pedro greeted them with a smile. "Glad you're here to help. Looks like someone went overboard with the decorations."

Rose laughed. "Are you talking about me, Pedro?" she asked innocently.

Juanita laughed with the others. She was not much older than Rose and was pleased that after years of being alone, Rose was now happily married.

Benjy came into the room and stood by as sparkly decorations were lifted out of bags and boxes. When Hank plugged a few strings of lights into electrical outlets, Benjy clapped his hands with glee.

Juanita watched it all—the group working together, the

way Rose took charge of the plan she'd drawn up, the delight on Benjy's face as the others fell into line, accepting direction from Hank and Rose, who were masters of design.

The dining room came alive with colors, shapes, smells, and light. Pine-scented fat candles sat in the center of each wooden table. Strung lights dipped and curved along the top of the walls, and in the far corner, a fireproof, fake Christmas tree stood, and was rapidly being filled with ornaments of every kind.

"Is that for me?" Benjy asked, taking hold of Juanita's hand and indicating the tree with a nod of his head.

"For you and everyone else who comes here," said Juanita.

"We have to have a place for Santa Claus to bring presents," said Willow, smiling at him.

Benjy shook his head from side to side, his lips stretched into a narrow line. "Santa Claus isn't comin'. Not for me."

The look of surprise on Willow's face was telling.

"We'll get it all sorted out later," Juanita said quietly. But then and there, she made a promise to herself that of all the problems that might arise going forward, this was a situation she intended to take care of in the best way she knew how.

CHAPTER FOUR

JUANITA

When Juanita pulled up in front of the Kitchen at 8 AM, a couple of her staffers were in the parking lot, waiting to go inside.

Natasha waved at her and smiled. Natasha Ivanov was a beautiful, forty-five-year-old Russian immigrant. Tall, with shiny brown hair she wore in a knot at the back of her head, she had bright-green eyes that were usually full of mystery. When she told Juanita and the Flowers the name Natasha in Russian meant Christmas Day, they were immediately intrigued. Divorced from a man who'd helped her get into the U.S. and then treated her as a slave, she'd worked cleaning houses for a while. Now, she was living alone in an apartment the charity had helped her find.

"This is such an exciting day," Natasha said as she accompanied Juanita to the front door.

"I'm hoping for a busy opening," said Juanita, unlocking the front door.

They stepped inside, and Lucita Ortiz, the oldest at fifty-two, quickly joined them. She'd had the care of her grandchildren since her daughter, a single mother, was caught up in a cycle of drugs that continued today. Thrilled to have her own larger apartment with the children, now seven and ten, Lucita was eager to help in any way she could.

"I said a prayer for today," Lucita said. "I know it's going to be a good one for us."

Juanita gave her a quick hug. "Thank you. How are the kids

doing on this Saturday morning? Your sister is staying with them?"

Lucita nodded happily. "They love *Tia* Carlotta. She's excited for all of us."

Ivy rushed down the stairs toward them. "Ah'm sorry, y'all, for not opening the door for you. Benjy and Ah overslept this morning after a restless night." She glanced at Juanita. "Too much excitement about Christmas."

Juanita didn't react. Somehow, she'd get through to Ivy that the Christmas spirit was the best part of the holiday season, if only to demonstrate the joy of giving.

Isaac showed up, followed by Rosita, and finally Summer Hunter, the last of the staff members to appear.

Summer was as interesting as the others. Of medium height and with a pleasantly round figure, Summer had pretty blue eyes and straight blond hair that reached her shoulders. As soon as she'd turned eighteen, she escaped her family home on the coast where her parents were heavily involved with drugs, providing a chaotic home life that tore at her with the changing moods of the people inside. Apparently, her parents knew where she was but never contacted her unless it was to ask for money. Now, at twenty-four, she was living in the area with her boyfriend, who seemed a sweet, kind man involved in a mental health program.

"Okay, now that everyone is here, let's get started on food preparation," said Juanita.

"Summer, you're taking care of setting up the dining room, right?" Ivy said, giving her a smile.

Summer nodded. "Got it covered." Paper plates would be used occasionally. But to keep to environment-friendly procedures, plastic melamine dishware was to be used, along with stainless silverware. In lieu of regular glassware, disposables were being used for both hot and cold drinks for sanitary purposes and to allow guests to take them with them.

Tables were covered with different colored vinyl cloths creating a rainbow of colors in the dining room. They, along with the new Christmas decorations made the room seem a holiday wonderland.

Today's offerings were a hearty vegetable soup, chicken and noodle casserole, and a favorite, chicken taco recipe Juanita had shown the staff how to make. Tossed salad, rolls and bread were available, along with a variety of fruit, cakes, and cookies for dessert.

Willow arrived and stood with Juanita off to the side watching the staff working under Ivy's supervision. "Smells delicious already. How are you doing?"

Tears stung Juanita's eyes. "I've been thinking of Alec all day."

"He'd be so happy to know we actually pulled off this idea. I know it's going to be a success." Willow smiled at her but couldn't hide the moisture in her own eyes.

As the morning progressed and the parking lot began to fill with people, Juanita and the others were relieved. She noticed a few people who looked as if they might not really need free food, but as they'd all decided earlier, there would be no judgement. Anyone who appeared would be fed.

As requested, a photographer and reporter from one of the local newspapers showed up and then another reporter from a local magazine. Rose and Lily appeared and stood by as photos of Juanita and the staff were taken.

After the reporters left, Juanita signaled the Flowers to join her in a private corner of the dining room.

"I think we need to take a moment to remember Alec and to thank him for this opportunity," Juanita said solemnly.

They formed a circle, held hands, and bowed their heads.

"Though you're not with us, we feel your love every day.

Thank you," Juanita whispered, ending their moment of silence.

"Okay, ladies, let's do this," said Rose. "Time to open the doors."

Juanita hurried to the kitchen, while the Flowers positioned themselves by the door.

Rose unlocked it and flung the door open with a flourish.

A group of about twenty people of different ages surged through the entrance and were directed to the service line to pick up their trays. Even as those patrons were being served, more people arrived.

Juanita was happy to see a number of children in the group. After seeing the kitchen staff had everything under control, she returned to the dining room to see how well the cafeteria-style service was going.

Standing by the door, Rose and Willow were talking quietly about different space arrangements when Juanita joined them. Lily was sitting behind a table at the back of the room where a number of brochures about various social services were displayed.

Juanita peered out the door to see who else might be coming. Her eyes widened when a small, elderly woman with white hair approached, walking carefully. The woman entered the dining room, stopped, and posed as if she was making an entrance on stage. Beaming, dressed in black flats and a pink polyester pantsuit, the woman straightened her fur stole around her shoulders, adjusted the large black bag she was carrying, and turned to Juanita.

"Darling, thank you so much for inviting me to lunch," the woman said. "It's been such a long time since anyone has asked me to dine."

"We're delighted you could be here," said Juanita, playing along with her.

Willow came over. "Hello. I'm Willow Sanchez. And you are?"

"Oh, dear. You're too young to remember. I'm Maribelle McGrath. Back in the day, everyone knew my name from my roles on stage and screen."

"Maribelle, if I may call you that, may I show you to your seat?" said Willow, her dark eyes twinkling with amusement as she held out her elbow.

Before they could walk away, Rose and Lily joined them.

After introductions were made, Rose said, "I'd be happy to help you with your tray."

"Why, that would be lovely," said Maribelle. "It's become quite difficult for me to get around like I used to."

After observing the others take off, Lily turned to Juanita. "How old do you think Maribelle is?"

"Even with the makeup she's wearing, she appears to be at least in her eighties and very fragile. We'll need to keep an eye on her. We don't want anything to happen to her here where she might get jostled."

"How did she get here?" said Lily, poking her head out the door to check the parking lot. "I don't see any vehicles that might be hers."

Juanita stepped away from the door to allow a few new guests inside and then peered out. She saw an old, white convertible, a Cadillac she thought, parked down the street. A young man emerged from the car and headed toward them.

Juanita elbowed Lily. "I think the answer is coming our way."

They waited together for the young man to approach.

"Good afternoon," Juanita said.

"Are you here for a meal?" asked Lily.

The handsome young man shook his head. "I just wanted to make sure that Ms. McGrath made it inside okay. She insisted I drop her off and park away from the entrance so others wouldn't see her battered old car."

"She's here and in good hands," Juanita assured him. "Won't you come in and join her for a nice, hot meal?"

Looking embarrassed, the young man nodded. "Thank you. By the way, I'm Jake Carter, Ms. McGrath's neighbor. We live in the same apartment building, and I sort of keep an eye on her. In exchange for me using her car, I drive her on errands and such."

"Does she have any family?" Juanita asked, curious in spite of herself.

Jake shook his head. "No. There's no one else. At one time she was a famous actress. Now, she has almost nothing. She's a sweet lady who still lives in a world that doesn't really exist, but I'm not going to burst her bubble. I just want her to be happy, you know?"

Juanita's eyes blinked rapidly to erase the sting of tears. "I do know. You remind me so much of a dear friend who helped us put together Juanita's Kitchen. Come inside and enjoy a nice hot meal."

Jake paused a moment, studied the decorations hanging on the wall and the Christmas tree in the corner, then bobbed his head. "Thanks. I will."

CHAPTER FIVE
IVY

Ivy looked up from serving the soup as another person stood before her. Staring into eyes that were a shade of turquoise, words stuck in her throat. Annoyed with herself for even noticing, she snapped, "Soup?"

The handsome, young blond man looked startled and then nodded. "Hey, aren't you in the culinary program at College of the Desert?"

"Yeah. So?" Ivy forced a neutral tone.

He smiled at her. "I thought I'd seen you there. I'm in the program too." He took the bowl she handed him and set it on his tray. "I didn't know you worked here. Cool. I'll have to come often, so we can meet up."

Clamping her teeth together to keep from responding, Ivy simply nodded and turned to the next person in line. Guys thought all it would take for her to fall into bed with them were corny lines like that. They didn't know she had no intention of being taken for a sucker again.

The guy she'd been dating in high school had told her he loved her, said he'd help her leave town, that they'd go off together and start a new life. When he found out she was pregnant, he'd freaked out and went back to his friends on the right side of town. And when she didn't agree to an abortion, he cut her off completely. Her parents were worse. They wished more than anything that neither she nor Benjy existed to mar their image of upright, religious citizens. Left alone, she'd moved in with a neighbor who'd taken pity on her. But as soon as she finished her high school classes and graduated, she took off with the sweet little boy she loved like no other. It had been that way ever since—the two of them facing life's challenges.

CHAPTER SIX
JUANITA

Juanita was busy observing the clean-up of the serving line when she noticed Maribelle, sitting alone, remove a plastic container from her black bag and carefully scrape food left on her plate into it. A pang of understanding gripped her. Jake must not have been exaggerating when he'd said that Maribelle was in difficult circumstances. She wondered how else she could help. Paper sacks filled with sandwiches were offered at the end of the serving line. Juanita walked over to Maribelle and sat down beside her.

"Did you enjoy your meal?" she asked politely.

Maribelle gave her a wide smile. "It was divine. It makes such a difference to be out and about, rather than sitting alone and being served at home. I'm so glad I saw the notice at church about this place." She patted Juanita's hand. "You're the person behind Juanita's Kitchen, aren't you?"

Juanita nodded. "The three other women you met and I are responsible for setting it up with the generosity of Alec Thurston, who used to own the Desert Sage Inn."

Maribelle's face brightened. "I went there once. Years ago, when it was new. I used to be quite well-known in the area, you understand."

Juanita smiled at her. "I'm sure you were."

"Ah, yes. Such good times. Fred Astaire was such a wonderful dancer. I danced with him once. A long time ago." Her lips curved. "It was a publicity stunt, but still quite wonderful."

Juanita caught Ivy's eye and waved her over. "Ivy, I want you to meet Ms. Maribelle McGrath. We're hoping she comes here often, and I want you to be sure she gets her bag of goodies to take home."

"Goodies? How wonderful?" She held out her hand to Ivy. "And you, my dear, are a very beautiful young woman."

Ivy took Maribelle's hand and smiled. "Nice to meet you."

Jake walked up to them. "What's going on? Anything I can do for you, Ms. McGrath?"

"Ah, Jake, here you are." She smiled at Ivy. "This young man is like the son I never had, a gentleman through and through. And Jake, dear, this is Ivy. Ivy ..."

"Ivy Barrett," she said.

"She goes to the culinary school at the College of the Desert, like me," he said.

Maribelle clapped her hands. "How perfect. I've been telling Jake he needs to get out more, have more fun. Poor boy works hard taking care of me and the apartment building we live in."

Juanita noticed the flicker of interest in Ivy's eyes but it disappeared as quickly as it had arrived. She didn't know what had happened to Benjy's father, but was aware that Ivy was no fan of men in general. When she and the Flowers had tried to talk to her about entertaining guests alone in the rooms upstairs after hours, she'd scoffed and said, "No problem. That's not ever going to happen."

Ivy said, "Why don't I bring goodie bags for both of you?"

"I'll get them," said Jake. He turned to Ivy. "Listen, while I was waiting for Ms. McGrath to finish eating, I talked to Willow Sanchez about the Premio Inn, the hotel she manages. I might apply for part-time work in the catering department. She's a good contact for students like us."

"Nice," said Ivy, before she turned and walked away.

As Jake left to get the sandwich bags, Juanita turned to Maribelle. "Jake is such a sweet young man. Does he have family here?"

Maribelle shook her head sadly. "His parents and sister died in an automobile accident a few years ago. I think he's still troubled by it, which is why I like to keep him close."

Surprised and touched by her words, Juanita just nodded. She'd always found it interesting that beneath the surface most people showed, they had such interesting stories. In this case, both Maribelle and Jake needed each other.

"Jake is managing the apartment complex?" Juanita asked.

Maribelle nodded. "He does that so he has a place to live and doesn't have to pay rent. He's a smart, ambitious young man. Reminds me of my Henry."

"Ready, Ms. McGrath?" said Jake approaching. "I'll go get the car and pick you up."

Maribelle nodded. "Thanks, dear. Such a shame about my car."

Jake chuckled softly and left the room.

Juanita and Rose helped Maribelle to the door and waited with her for Jake to pull up with Maribelle's car. As soon as Juanita saw it, she understood Jake's quiet laughter. The old car looked as if it had been in a demolition derby. Dents on both sides of the fenders front and back told a story of their own. Juanita wondered how long Maribelle had been driving before she no longer could.

Maribelle turned to her. "The car and I have had a few adventures, but I'd never get rid of it. Jack Warner Jr. gave it to me years ago for being in one of his movies."

Jake hurried over to them. With a quiet gentleness, he took Maribelle's arm, carefully led her to the car, and helped her into it.

Lily and Willow joined Juanita and Rose at the door and

watched Jake pull out of the driveway and into the street.

"What an interesting pair," said Rose. "Willow and I talked to Jake, and he seems to have his act put together."

"Yes," said Willow. "I was very impressed by him. I told him to come and apply for a job at the Premio. He wants to go into the catering business."

"Did you know he and Ivy are attending school together?" said Juanita.

"Really?" said Lily. "They'd make such an adorable couple."

Juanita shook her head. "You're a hopeless romantic, though I did notice a spark of interest in Ivy. But she quickly shut it down."

"How do you think everything went today?" Rose asked her.

"Very well. Though the dining room wasn't filled, it was a pretty steady stream of people." Juanita glanced around. "The staff is doing great at cleaning up."

"Let's go celebrate with them," said Willow.

Juanita led the way into the kitchen. The last of the cleanup was underway. The rule was the kitchen was to be scrubbed thoroughly after each meal.

"Congratulations to you all," Juanita announced. "Our first day was a success."

"I'd like to add my thanks," said Rose. "From the sound of it, everyone enjoyed their meals."

"The people I talked to on the way out said they were coming back and would bring friends," said Lily, beaming at the staff.

"Job well done," said Willow, joining in.

"Take a break tomorrow, then on Monday, our real test begins when we do six straight days," said Juanita. "Ivy, do you have anything to say?"

Ivy nodded and said, "Great job, y'all. We can do this!" She raised a fist into the air.

Amid the clapping that followed, Lily said, "I'm going home and taking a nap." She gave Juanita and the other two Flowers a hug and left.

"I'm leaving too," said Rose. "But I'll be back early Monday morning before the staff arrives. I've made arrangements to work with Ivy on marketing figures."

"I promised Craig I'd help with a project at the house. See you later, Mom." Willow kissed her goodbye and left with the others.

Standing alone, Juanita glanced at her staff preparing to leave. They'd worked well together, a real team. And not just because of the paycheck. She knew how important it was to have this kind of cooperation. She'd learned that from years of being close to Alec, hearing about his business. Funny, how much she remembered about it when working at the Kitchen.

She heard her name being called and turned as Pedro and Benjy entered the room. Benjy ran toward her exclaiming, "Papa Pedro and Ah are workin' on surprises." After wondering about names to use, Ivy had agreed Benjy could call him Papa Pedro.

"Surprises?" Juanita laughed and hugged Benjy to her. "You are?"

Benjy nodded. "But I can't tell anyone about them. Even you."

Pedro gave her a wide grin. "We've had quite a day. How did it go here?"

Juanita and Ivy exchanged glances. "Ivy, why don't you tell him?"

A smile crept across Ivy's face. "It was a big success." She indicated the other staff members standing behind her with a wave of her hand. "We all did great!"

"*Bueno*," said Pedro. "Good job, everyone."

"Mama," said Benjy, waving a fist in the air. "Ah lak it heah."

Everyone chuckled at the way Benjy's southern accent showed up when he was excited.

"Ready to go?" Pedro asked her as the other staff members headed out the door.

"Yes," Juanita replied and faced Ivy. "Thank you for a good day."

"See you later," Ivy said quietly, but her eyes were alight with pleasure as she placed an arm around Benjy.

CHAPTER SEVEN
IVY

Ivy followed Juanita and Pedro to the door and locked it behind them. She was still tingling with excitement over their first day at the Kitchen. She'd seen how the staff had responded when she gave clear, direct instructions to them. It was something she'd learned to do in one of her classes. Having the day go so well kept the dream of someday opening a restaurant seem a real possibility.

The attendees had seemed a nice group, fairly quiet and appreciative. She especially liked seeing the children in line. She was proud of the fact that though she'd scraped and scrimped by on her own, she'd always managed to feed Benjy well. Working in restaurants and at resorts made it easier for her than others, but still, it was a point of pride. Her thoughts flew to Jake Carter. Maybe she'd been too sharp with him. After seeing how sweet he was to Maribelle, that funny old woman, he didn't seem like such a jerk. But if Maribelle or others thought there'd be something romantic between them, they were wrong. The only way she was going to fulfill her dreams was by working hard—and alone.

She felt a tug on her apron and looked down.

Benjy smiled up at her. "Mama, can Ah have this Christmas star for my room?"

"Where did you get that?" Ivy asked, unable to stop a frown from crossing her brow.

"It was on the Christmas tree," he said. "But Ah want a decoration for my room."

Ivy sighed. One of the things she treasured about her relationship with Benjy was her honesty with him. She knew if she wasn't totally honest about everything, he might get hurt. Life sometimes sucked. That's just the way it was.

"Listen, Benjy, Ah know you like all the colorful lights and glitter and all, but Ah don't want you to get carried away with the idea of this being a Christmas when Santa Claus arrives with a bundle of gifts for you. That's not how it works with you and me. It never has been."

He gave her a thoughtful look, staring into her eyes until she looked away. "One little Christmas star is all Ah want," he said quietly. "Ah know about how Santa isn't coming."

Pain pricked Ivy. She hated taking away dreams from him, but sometimes it was the fairest thing. "Tell you what, Benjy. You can hang that star in your room. Ah'll even help you."

His wide smile stung her eyes.

Benjy headed for the stairs and Ivy followed. She didn't like being so strict with him, but she'd learned her lessons the hard way. As she was growing up, Christmas Day had been one long church service followed by a roast turkey that tasted as bad as it looked because her mother's cooking was as devoid of tenderness as she herself was. Santa Claus was thought of as a way for stores to trick customers into spending their money, not an acceptable celebration in their house. And later, on her own without enough funds to make a big deal of it, she decided not to celebrate the Christmas season at all.

Now, with all these wonderful people around her, she wasn't so sure.

CHAPTER EIGHT
JUANITA

Juanita and Pedro left the Kitchen and climbed into Pedro's truck. It had been an exhausting day for her, but a worthwhile one.

"How did it go with Benjy?" she asked Pedro. It had done her heart good to see him racing toward her.

Pedro chuckled. "He's a lively one all right. But I kept him pretty busy in my woodworking shop. And before you say anything, I watched him closely and showed him why it was so important not to touch any tools without my help. I also gave him my iPad to play a game. He's a bright boy."

"Yes, he is," said Juanita feeling a bit of pride. She wondered what it would be like when Willow and Craig presented them with grandchildren. From the sound of it, it wouldn't be anytime soon.

"Are you happy with the way the day went?" Pedro asked.

Juanita felt a smile spread across her face. "Alec would've been so proud of what we've done today. The staff did a wonderful job. But, as I told them, the real test will be next week."

"I'm sure they'll do fine," said Pedro, giving her hand a squeeze. "Let's relax and enjoy the evening. I'm pooped."

Juanita laughed. He looked as exhausted as she felt. She knew from her afternoons alone with Benjy how much energy it took to keep him occupied.

###

That evening, Willow and Craig surprised them with a visit. Juanita rose from the couch to greet them at the door. "Hello, you two. Come in. Come in."

Willow gave her a kiss on the cheek. "Hope you don't mind our popping in like this."

"You know I love it," Juanita answered happily.

"Thanks, Mrs. Sanchez," said Craig following her into the living room and sitting in a chair near the couch. "Willow and I want to talk to you about the wedding plans. We've changed the venue for the rehearsal dinner to Tico's. My father, along with Loretta and Ricardo Morales, are going to host it. Loretta has taken on the role of mother with me after my own mother passed, and she and Ricardo wanted to be part of it. We hope you agree that this makes sense. We were able to pull a few strings to reserve a private room."

"I know with all the help Rose and Lily have been giving me with the wedding that you've been feeling left out. That's why we've come to you with this change," said Willow.

"The two of you deserve to have the wedding of your choice, including the rehearsal dinner," Juanita replied. "It's being together as a family that matters." She glanced at Pedro and back to them. "In this case, we couldn't be happier with your choices. Craig, we've known your father for years, as well as Loretta and Ricardo. It's a wonderful blend of families."

"Oh, thank you, *Mami!*" cried Willow. "That means so much to us."

"Yes, Mr. and Mrs. Sanchez, we want everyone to be happy," said Craig.

"Well, then, you have to do one more thing," said Juanita, smiling playfully at them. "I think it's time for you, Craig, to call us by our given names, Juanita and Pedro."

Craig returned her smile and said, "Okay, I'll try to remember."

"Thank you for that, both of you," said Willow, her eyes suspiciously moist. "That's a request that had to come from the two of you. It makes me very happy."

Pedro rose and shook hands with Craig. "It's nice to have a son after all these years."

Juanita's heart filled with love for her husband and for the young man who, she knew, would treat her daughter well.

When talk about Pedro's woodworking shop turned into an invitation from Pedro for Craig to see it, Willow signaled Juanita. "C'mon. Let's see what you intend to wear to the rehearsal dinner. It won't be as fancy as the one we'd planned earlier at the Premio Inn."

Juanita led Willow into her bedroom. After years of wearing a black skirt and white blouse to work, she'd enjoyed shopping for more exciting clothes. In the last few months since Alec died, she'd lost some weight. Enough to make a difference. And with Willow acting as an advisor, she had a pretty decent selection from which to choose.

She strode to her closet, opened it, and said, "Okay, what do you think?"

Giggling as she tried on one dress after another, she and Willow chatted about the bridesmaid dresses the other two Flowers had chosen. Each one was wearing a different style in the same rich green that set off both their hair color and skin tones beautifully. Though Lily had been forced to accommodate her baby bump, her two-piece outfit, a skirt and adjustable top went well with Rose's classic sleeveless dress.

After they quickly decided on a turquoise dress for the rehearsal dinner, Willow pulled another one out of the closet.

"I wanted to see this again. It's so perfect for the wedding," said Willow, holding onto a hanger on which Juanita's dress hung. A pretty, quarter-sleeve, tea-length dress in a deep red silk, it spoke of good taste with its classic, smooth lines.

Everyone had agreed it fit Juanita perfectly, as if it was made for her.

"It's going to be a beautiful wedding," Juanita said happily, as Willow hung up the dress she adored.

"I hope so. I guess every bride worries about her wedding," Willow said. "The only thing I'm not worried about is Craig. He makes me so happy."

Juanita hugged her. "My darling, all any mother hopes for is for her children to be happy. Craig is a good man, like your father."

"He told me he's really missing his mother right now," Willow said softly.

"Well, then, I'll have to help him out however I can," she said. "That's the thing about love. There's always enough to go around."

Willow looked at her with tears in her eyes. "I love you, *Mami,*" she said, giving her mother a hug.

Feeling so grateful to have Willow in her life, Juanita hugged her back.

After a day of rest, Juanita drove to the Kitchen with fresh energy. The talk with Willow had gone well and had made her see she needn't feel useless, that other people were counting on her to be there for them. And it felt good.

The building was quiet when she walked inside. She'd seen Rose's car outside and knew she and Ivy were scheduled to go over marketing and inventory figures. She climbed the stairs to the office eager to learn for herself how the actual inventory compared to the projected one. They had to keep a careful line between having too many supplies on hand and not having enough. They'd been able to get special bulk pricing on goods, and they'd applied for funding from the state and local government, but they had to watch every penny. Fundraising plans were already underway.

As she reached the top of the landing, she automatically checked Benjy's room and stopped in surprise. "Benjy, what are you doing home?" she asked, approaching his bed. "Shouldn't you be in school?"

"Ah got a cold," he said, giving her an unhappy look and promptly sneezing.

"Oh, my! I'm sorry. I have to check on a few things. But why don't I check on you later to see how you're doing?" She noted the glass of water by his bed and a plate with some toast on it.

"Will you read to me?" Benjy said, holding up the book he'd had in his lap.

"After I make certain things are up and running in the kitchen," she left him and entered the office. "Good morning! I see our little guy is down with a cold."

Ivy nodded. "I'm letting him stay home from school today."

"Very wise," Juanita said. "I agreed to read a story to Benjy, but first, I want to make sure everything is set for the day."

"Come join us, Juanita," said Rose. "We're reworking our inventory requirements based on our first day."

"We had a total of sixty-two people over the 3-hour time period," said Ivy. "If we go to full capacity, it could be three times that number or more."

"We're trying to project how long it would take to reach that goal," Rose said. "Based on Saturday's attendance and the feedback we received we're guessing sometime within two weeks. Word travels fast in some circles. And now with the newspaper and magazine coverage we're getting, the news will travel even faster."

"How does this affect staffing? Rose, you're in charge of setting up a volunteer group. How's that looking?" asked Juanita.

"Actually, I'm scheduling training sessions each day this week so we'll have at least twenty volunteers standing by and ready to go when the time comes. That's just the beginning."

Juanita loved how Rose, Willow, and Lily were so capable, so thorough. "Are you going to be able to handle training of the staff with Rose?" she asked Ivy.

Ivy nodded. "Yes. The other staff members will also be there to assist."

"Sounds good. I'll go downstairs and get ready for the others." As she left the room, she waved at Benjy. "I'll be back as soon as I can."

Downstairs, she turned on the lights and opened the door. Staff members filed inside. She greeted them cheerily, then said, "Where's Lucita?"

She checked her phone and found a message from her. *"I've got a terrible migraine. Will be a little late."*

Worried, Juanita called her. "Good morning. I got your message. Sorry to hear you're not feeling well."

"I want to come in, I really do, but I've been so nauseous from the pain I'm not sure I'll make it," Lucita said in a weak voice. "I'll try. I don't want to let you down."

"Don't worry about today. Better for you to rest." Juanita said. "Thanks for letting us know." She hung up the phone wondering if this was how it was going to be.

When Rose and Ivy joined her in the kitchen, she told them about Lucita and said, "I'll do Lucita's work in kitchen prep."

"I can help serve," said Rose. "In fact, I'll have one of my volunteers help me. No time like the present to get them started. But I won't be able to come in every day. Hank and I are starting a new consulting project for a business based out of Seattle."

"I understand," Juanita said. "We set up the Kitchen knowing you and the other two Flowers would not be available to help with the cooking and serving except for emergencies. But I do think staffing with volunteers is going to be a big help."

"I'll help cover for Lucita in the kitchen," said Ivy. "And we'll do as much prepping for tomorrow's meals as possible, to try and keep ahead of the schedule."

"Good idea," said Juanita.

"I've got to run," said Rose. "I'll be back just before noon with a volunteer."

Juanita saw her off and then helped Ivy gather the ingredients for the veggie soup they were going to make and set Isaac and Rosita to chopping.

Natasha was cleaning the lettuce for a green salad, and Summer was working on egg salad sandwiches, when Isaac yelped and held up a bloody hand.

Juanita hurried over to him just as he collapsed on the floor. Heart pounding, she knelt beside him. "Isaac, are you all right?"

He stirred and sat up. Giving her a sheepish look, he said, "It's the blood. It makes me faint." He held out his bloody left hand and closed his eyes.

Ivy tossed Juanita a clean kitchen towel and Juanita wrapped it around Isaac's hand. She'd seen enough to realize that the blood was coming from a deep, clean cut on one of his fingers.

"Do you feel well enough to stand? I think we should take you to emergency care so they can take a look at it."

With both Juanita and Ivy steadying him, Isaac was able to stand.

"I'm sorry," he said. "I forgot to put on my safety glove. I've never been able to tolerate the sight of blood. Especially since I came back from the war."

Juanita patted his arm. "You're going to be fine. I'll take

you to an emergency center close by so they can look at it." Isaac had lost color in his face and was still a bit wobbly, but she'd seen that though the cut was deep, no arteries were involved. Still, stitches appeared to her to be a good idea.

As she helped Isaac to her car, she was thankful that Ivy, the Flowers, and she had all recently taken a first aid course. They also carried special health insurance for their employees.

Later, sitting in the waiting room while someone was looking after Isaac's wound, Juanita wondered how the day that had started on such a bright note had changed so quickly. One thing was for certain. The sooner they had a crew of volunteers helping, the better.

After what seemed an inordinate amount of time, Juanita drove Isaac to his sister's house, explained the situation, and said that Isaac could come to work tomorrow.

She arrived back at the Kitchen just as Rose pulled her car into the parking lot with another woman and waited to greet them.

"I'm very happy you're here," Juanita said, smiling. "We've had a bit of a rough morning."

Rose introduced her to Sylvia Corcoran and listened as Juanita explained what had happened.

"Now, let's make sure we're ready to open," Juanita added.

As they went inside, Juanita wasn't sure what to expect. When she saw food being put out to be served and the dining room ready for guests, she was filled with relief.

In the kitchen, Ivy's face was flushed as she pulled a tray of cookies out of the oven. With her rosy cheeks, blond hair, and blue eyes, she'd never looked or seemed more like an angel.

"Thank you!" Juanita gushed. "It looks like everything is under control."

Ivy nodded. "Kitchen accidents happen all the time. We'll have to put Isaac to work doing things other than chopping.

And safety gloves are a must for everyone doing that kind of work."

Juanita couldn't help herself. She threw her arms around Ivy. "You're wonderful."

Ivy's body stiffened, then slowly relaxed enough for Juanita to give her a last pat on the back. Someday Ivy would believe just how special she was.

"It's a very nice set-up," said Sylvia coming into the kitchen with Rose after touring the property. "I think this is going to be fun."

Juanita handed her a T-shirt, an apron, and a pair of latex gloves. "Better get ready. Here comes our first guest."

CHAPTER NINE
IVY

Ivy stayed in the kitchen loading half pans for the hot buffet items and thinking about Juanita. She'd never met anyone quite like her. Not only had she taken Benjy under her wing, acting more like a grandmother to him than he'd ever known, she continually told Ivy how good she was at her job, with her school work, and as a mother. In the past, people like that had annoyed her with their overly cheery compliments. But Juanita was different. She seemed to mean all the kind things she said.

As it got busier, Rose and the new volunteer, Sylvia, helped her keep the serving line well stocked.

She glanced around. "Where's Juanita?"

"With Benjy," said Rose. "She took some soup and crackers up to him," Rose said smiling. "She really loves that boy of yours."

"Yes, I know," Ivy said.

Rose smiled at her. "It's good for Juanita to have him around. Following Alec's death and with Willow's wedding coming up, she's seemed a little down."

Ivy let that thought settle. Since she had been hired and moved into the rooms above the Kitchen, Benjy seemed happier than he'd ever been. She too was feeling more settled. A lot of it had to do with the loving, kind woman and her husband who kept protective watch over them as if they were part of their family.

CHAPTER TEN

JUANITA

As Juanita carried the tray holding the dirty dishes from Benjy's room down the stairs, she took a moment to study the group in the dining room. A sprinkling of mothers sat with their toddlers. Most of the occupants at the tables were older men. Some were dressed in decent clothing. Others were not. And like a ray of sunshine among them, Maribelle McGrath, wearing a bright yellow outfit, sat quietly eating her food.

Juanita looked for Jake but didn't see him.

After delivering the tray to the kitchen, Juanita went out to the dining room to visit with Maribelle. She'd had a chance to look up Maribelle's name on the internet and was intrigued by what she'd read. Maribelle was indeed well-known—as the mistress of a famous movie star back in the sixties. It was a sad story. They'd met while working together doing theater and stayed together for years. Even though the star's wife continued to be institutionalized, he and Maribelle never married.

Maribelle smiled and looked up as Juanita took a seat beside her. "Good afternoon, my dear. Thank you for another wonderful meal."

"I'm glad you're here," said Juanita returning her smile.

"It's the highlight of my day," said Maribelle, patting her mouth delicately with her paper napkin. "But I'll have to be careful not to eat too much. For my figure, you know."

Juanita patted her hand. "You may have as much as you

want. I don't see Jake. Is he here?"

Maribelle shook her head. "He dropped me off but couldn't stay."

"Do you need a ride home?" asked Juanita, concerned about Maribelle's ability to walk any distance.

Maribelle smiled, crinkling the corners of her bright blue eyes even more. "That would be so lovely. The dear boy had to handle a problem at the apartment building."

"I'll be happy to drive you. Let me know when you're ready." Juanita had noticed an empty plastic container sticking out of Maribelle's black bag, and wanting to give her some privacy, she rose and walked away.

At the table with flyers and other informational packets for their guests, she noticed not many had been taken. Maybe there was a better way to get the helpful information out to the people who came to eat. Perhaps a guest speaker? It was something she'd talk over with the Flowers.

A young girl approached. "May I have one?"

Smiling, Juanita nodded. "Of course. Help yourself." Before she could ask her name, the girl took a brochure and trotted over to a gray-haired woman who was heading toward her using a walker.

"Hello," Juanita said, greeting the older woman with a smile. "We're glad you could come. Don't forget your goodie bags to take with you."

"Oh, yes. That's so nice. Dori, run and get them," said the woman, motioning to the young girl.

As Dori ran toward the serving line, the older woman pressed Juanita's hand between her own two. "Thank you so much for being part of Juanita's Kitchen. It makes a huge difference not only to me, but to all the others here."

Touched, Juanita said, "I'm glad we can do this." She felt Alex's approval within her.

Dori returned holding two brown paper bags. "Here, Grandma. I'll hold them for you."

"Thank you. Come. Our ride should be outside."

Juanita walked with them to the doorway and saw a community van waiting there. A man stood by, ready to help them inside.

After the van left, Juanita stayed by the door, greeting people as they arrived and left. When they'd first talked about the Kitchen, Juanita had assumed that many of those who came to eat would be people living on the street. But that wasn't necessarily the case. Some were mothers with small children, who, she suspected, might be homeless but often found a place to stay for the night. Others were older, nicely dressed people who, perhaps, had lost jobs or were living on inadequate social security funds or enduring tough times for other reasons. Mental problems or alcohol abuse were sometimes issues. Many guests came and left quickly. Others stayed, enjoying the warmth or, like Maribelle, the company.

More than ever, Juanita was grateful for Alec and how his generosity was being used to help people. He'd often been referred to as a superb hotelier. She loved that even after he was gone, his hospitality was continuing in this new way.

Maribelle came over to her. "I'm ready to go now, if you're still able to take me home."

"Sure. Let me tell Ivy and Rose we're leaving. Then I'll grab my coat and purse, and we'll be on our way."

A few minutes later, Juanita led Maribelle to her car.

Following Maribelle's directions, Juanita drove to a building in an older neighborhood in the downtown area. The tan-adobe building with red-tile roofing was two stories high, with what looked like twelve apartments on each floor. Though the sidewalks in front of the first-floor apartments were cracked, and the outside walls of the building were in desperate need of paint, sidewalks were swept, the patches of green grass by each door were mowed and edged, and pots of flowers and decorative items sat by many entrances. Number 6, Maribelle's apartment, had a floral wreath hanging on the door.

"Here we are," Maribelle said cheerfully. "A lot different from what I'd become accustomed to, but it's not too bad inside." Juanita smiled and nodded, hiding her dismay.

Jake appeared around the corner of the building and jogged over to her car. "Hi, Mrs. Sanchez. Sorry I couldn't stay for lunch, but I had to hang around and wait for a plumber to show up." He went to Maribelle's car door and held it open.

Maribelle smiled up at him. "Don't you worry, Jake. I brought home enough food for us both." She handed him the brown paper bags she'd picked up at the Kitchen.

He grinned. "Thanks. Let me help you to your apartment." He gently assisted her out of the car, took her elbow, and closed the passenger door behind them.

Watching the two of them slowly make their way to Maribelle's front door, Juanita filled with emotion. They were the sweetest of friends.

Juanita returned to the Kitchen to find the staff busy cleaning up. She approached Ivy. "How did it go?"

Ivy shrugged. "Good. I think having Rose and a volunteer helped a lot. But without two of our regular staff, it was touch and go for a while. That's why I wanted to get things ready for tomorrow as much as possible."

"Good idea."

Juanita left the kitchen and approached Rose, who was stacking papers on the information table. "I have something I want to discuss with you. A new idea."

"Sure. What's up?" Rose asked.

Juanita told her about the idea of guest speakers.

Rose grinned. "That would be a great opportunity not only for our visitors but for promoting the Kitchen in the community. If you'd like, I can talk to some of the county and city agencies, and at the next board meeting, I will report back to you and the others."

"Wonderful," said Juanita, pleased with her response. Each new idea would build a better charity.

Over the next several days, Juanita grew more comfortable with Ivy handling the kitchen while she spoke to the people who came and went. After the first guest speaker, a woman from an alcohol recovery center, had spoken to the group and someone approached her, Juanita was pleased. The dream they'd had for the Kitchen was becoming even bigger.

As busy as she was at the Kitchen, Juanita's thoughts remained on the little boy who'd won her heart. She loved their afternoons together. As active as he normally was, he was content to make those times with her quiet ones.

One afternoon, looking quite serious, he said, "Nita, someone at school told me there's no Santa, that it's just parents giving you gifts. Is that right?"

Seeing Isaac out of the corner of her eyes, she waved him over. "Isaac, someone told Benjy there wasn't a Santa. What do you think?"

The big man knelt in front of the couch and looked straight into Benjy's eyes. "That's not true. Know why?"

Benjy shook his head and looked as if he was holding his breath.

"'Cause Santa is alive and well in each one of us. Yessir, that's what I believe."

Benjy looked down at his stomach. "But how does he fit in?"

Isaac laughed and ruffled Benjy's curls. "You'll see what I mean come Christmas Day. I believe that. I really do."

Juanita reached out and touched Isaac's arm. "What a lovely thought. Thank you."

Isaac rose and beamed at them. "You'll see, Benjy. I promise."

After Isaac left them, Benjy gave her a troubled look. "Is he right?"

"I believe he is," she said.

At the smile that spread across his face, a wave of happiness washed through her.

CHAPTER ELEVEN
IVY

One day, Ivy was walking across the campus of the College of the Desert when she heard someone call her name. She turned as Jake trotted up to her.

"Have a minute?" he said.

She shrugged and kept on walking. She liked him but she couldn't trust him or any man. Not after all the crap she'd been through,

Jake stayed at her side. "I just wanted to say thank you for helping Maribelle and me out. She loves coming to Juanita's Kitchen. It's good for her to be out with other people, and the food is delicious. Is that what you want to do? Continue working with food?"

Ivy was quiet and then said, "Yes, I was thinking of maybe owning a restaurant one day. It's something I've dreamed about for a long time. Being here at school is part of it."

"Cool. I want to have my own catering business," said Jake. "Maybe we could work together after we get our degrees."

She stopped and stared at him. Jake didn't get that she was a loner. "Why would you say something like that? You don't even know me."

He chuckled. "But I do. I see how you are at the Kitchen, working with others, making sure things go smoothly. I like that you can do that."

"Yeah? There's a lot more to it than you might think." Ivy couldn't hide her scorn. Anybody could run a kitchen, but to go into business with someone was a whole other story.

Rather than react to her dismissal of him, Jake just whistled and strolled at her side in long, sure steps. It rattled her. She hadn't told him to leave her alone, but still, she wasn't encouraging his company.

"How about a cup of coffee at the Grill?" Jake asked her. "My treat."

Ivy stopped and toed the sidewalk with her sneaker. He sounded so sincere, maybe a little lonely. "I don't know."

"Come on. It's just coffee. Between school and being caretaker at the apartments, I don't get time to chat with anyone my age. Give me a break." His smile was friendly with a light touch of humor she found intriguing.

She let out a long sigh. "Okay." She'd been feeling a bit out of touch with others, and she had time to kill before Juanita expected her back.

The Grill was busy when they walked inside but Ivy found a table in a back corner.

"What'll you have?"

Suddenly excited for a treat, Ivy said, "A grande latte."

Jake gave her a little salute and went to stand in line.

As she waited for Jake to return, Ivy looked around at the other people, mostly students. Every once in a while, it surprised her that she'd come this far. Sure, she'd had some luck in the past but mostly it was due to hard work, long hours, and a determination to be a better parent to Benjy than she'd ever known.

Jake returned and sitting and talking with him turned out to be a lot more interesting than Ivy had thought. She learned he was really serious about setting up a catering business. Later on, he might consider opening a restaurant, but catering would give him an entrée into the desert food business and the community at large.

"I have some money set aside for it," Jake said, the sparkle leaving his eyes. "An inheritance from when my parents and sister were killed."

"I'm so sorry. I didn't know. I don't have a good relationship with my family, but I can't imagine how difficult that must have been for you. And still is."

He looked off into the distance and let out a shaky breath. "Yeah, I don't usually talk about it. We were close. Saving money to open my own business is a way to honor them."

When he turned back to her, his eyes were full of a sorrow that tugged at her. "I want to do something useful with what I have left of them. I couldn't afford a bigger culinary program, but this will give me the start I need."

"Yeah, I'm going to make this count for me too," Ivy said, touched by his goal. "Having Benjy to take care of makes me want to do good things for him."

"I've seen him around the Kitchen," said Jake. "He seems like a good kid."

Ivy couldn't help the smile that spread across her face. "He is. Bright too. He's mah shinin' light, you know?"

Jake nodded. "I get it."

She checked her watch. "Speaking of him, I'd better go. Juanita watches him for me while I come here, but I don't want to take advantage of her."

"Juanita's a great person," said Jake. "She doesn't only offer meals; she spends time with Maribelle and some of the other guests. Maribelle loves her and the women that work with her."

"They're all pretty amazing. I wasn't sure about them in the beginning, but now I am," Ivy admitted.

Jake gave her a direct look. "Sometimes it's okay to trust others. Sometimes that's all you have."

Ivy studied him and nodded, wondering how he seemed to understand so much about her. Then she walked away.

CHAPTER TWELVE
JUANITA

As Juanita settled into her new, busy routine, she felt happier, more useful than she had in a long time. Most days, she and the Flowers took some time to spend with Maribelle, aware of her loneliness. Besides, talking with her was always interesting. She had quite a remarkable past.

When Juanita told her about Willow's upcoming wedding, Maribelle clasped her hands together and said, "Oh, I just LOVE weddings!"

Juanita smiled. "Me too. And this is going to be a small, beautiful one."

"I wish ... oh, never mind me," said Maribelle, letting her voice trail off, but Juanita knew what she wanted and, later, mentioned it to Willow.

Willow, sweet and kind as always, quickly suggested they invite Maribelle to the wedding. "Our wedding is small enough that she could easily attend the service and reception without it being a problem to add one more to the group."

"I think we should ask Jake too, so he can take care of her," said Juanita.

Willow gave her a devilish grin. "Then, let's invite Ivy. That might help the two of them get together. I've seen how they look at one another when they think no one else will see."

Juanita laughed. "You and Lily are incorrigible romantics. But maybe we can add a little Christmas magic to your wedding."

Willow gave her a high five, and they smiled together.

Later, when Willow and Juanita asked Maribelle together, Maribelle's eyes filled. "Oh, my dears! I never ... but, of course, I'd be only too delighted to come. There's something about a wedding that makes me believe love never ends." She dabbed at her eyes with a lacy handkerchief she pulled from her purse. "It makes me believe in my love for Henry."

Juanita gave her a hug. "In the meantime, we'll ask Jake to accompany you so you'll have a gentleman attending to you."

"You women are the sweetest ever." Maribelle's blue eyes sparkled with excitement. "An evening wedding you said? I have the perfect dress to wear."

Juanita chuckled softly, unable to imagine what Maribelle's outfit might be.

When Willow told her that Jake had agreed to come to the wedding as Maribelle's date, a warmth went through Juanita. Sweet Christmas surprises made the holiday special. But they both knew getting Ivy to agree to come would be trickier. Because of her nature, Ivy would be suspicious of their invitation. Willow and Juanita agreed to bide their time before asking her.

As the wedding drew closer, Juanita's excitement grew. Rose and Lily had planned a bridal shower for Willow for that evening at Rose's house, and she was looking forward to it. Guests had been requested to bring two different gifts— something serious and something fun.

Rose and Lily greeted her at the door and ushered her inside.

"We're glad you could come early so we can take pictures of you and Willow together and then more with the four of us," said Rose.

"If I can even fit into one," joked Lily, rubbing her

enormous stomach.

Willow came over to Juanita and gave her a kiss on the cheek. "Doesn't everything look lovely?"

Juanita studied the living room. The Christmas tree in the corner of the room was covered with tiny, white lights and shimmering silver ornaments of all sizes and shapes. The simple combination was stunning.

She noticed the white bows on boxes wrapped in silver and then the decorations in the dining room. Candles flickered in glass holders on either side of a silver pot filled with white poinsettias sitting in the center of the table. At one end of the table, a collection of cupcakes filled a tray, each one decorated with white icing and silver sugar sprinkles.

"Everything is beautiful," gushed Juanita. "I hope you took photos for your blog, Rose."

She ran an online blog called "You Deserve This" filled with ideas about travel, dining, entertaining, gifts, and things a young professional or homemaker might be interested in.

"Thank you, I did," Rose said. "I love the simple theme."

"Okay, let's get pictures of you and Willow," said Lily, waving them over to her. "Come stand by the table."

Juanita proudly stood next to her daughter. Willow had always been a striking child and woman, but this evening a glow of love brightened her features making her even more beautiful.

"As soon as one of our guests arrive, we can ask her to take pictures of the four of us," said Rose.

Everyone seemed to arrive at once, bubbling with excitement. The photo was pushed aside as drinks were handed out and people shared news with one another.

Juanita enjoyed it all.

And when it came time for Willow to open gifts, she sat as close to the action as possible, not wanting to miss anything.

As presents were opened, the predicable sounds of appreciation could be heard. And when a few of the fun gifts turned out to be sexy undergarments or negligees, laughter and sly comments made Juanita blush, but she joined in the fun. Her gift of lacy, black-silk panties and bra were tame compared to some.

The time flew as the wine flowed and food offerings were gobbled up.

At the end of the party, Willow thanked Rose and everyone for coming. "Just one more week until it's official," she said happily.

Guests filed out the door.

"Wait!" said Rose. "We need someone to take a picture of the four of us."

Sarah Jensen, who worked at the Desert Sage Inn as a part-time reservations clerk and was a dear friend to all of them, returned. "No problem. Where do you want to pose for the pictures?"

"How about next to the Christmas tree," said Rose.

Juanita joined the others by the tree, wrapped her arms around Lily next to her in line and dutifully said, "Cheese!" when prompted.

She felt Lily stiffen and turned to her.

Lily stared at her round-eyed and then her face crinkled with pain. "I'm having a contraction! Oh, my God! I think the baby might be coming!"

She waddled away from them.

Juanita and the others followed.

When Lily emerged from the bathroom, she announced. "My water's broken." She held her stomach and groaned.

"Oh my God! We'd better get her to the hospital," said Rose.

"Call Brian," Juanita said.

"I'll go to their house now so I can stay with the kids," said Willow. She turned and hugged Lily. "Good luck with everything. Love you."

Lily nodded and clamped her teeth against another pain.

"We'd better take her to the hospital now," said Juanita. "Since her water broke, it's been only a couple of minutes between pains. Brian can meet us there."

"Get some towels," said Rose. "I'll help her to the car."

Juanita grabbed her purse and Lily's, and they headed outside to her car.

Rose met them, spread some towels on the back seat, and stood by. "There! I'll sit in back with you, Lily. Juanita, you drive."

Juanita was normally a cautious driver. But now, she drove as if she was on the nearby off-road raceway. First babies were usually slow, but Lily wasn't showing any signs of that. The moans from the backseat were continuing proof of it.

She pulled up at the Desert Regional Medical Center emergency entrance and braked to a stop, feeling as if she'd been in the biggest race of her life.

Rose ran inside to get help, and within seconds, a wheelchair was brought out for Lily. Juanita left Rose and Lily and went searching for a parking spot.

When Brian arrived at the room assigned to Lily, his face was flushed with excitement. He gave them a quick wave and headed for Lily's side.

"It's going to be okay," he said to Lily. "I'm here."

"Should we stay?" Rose whispered.

"Why don't we go home," Juanita said. "I'm sure they'll call us when they're ready to share the news."

"You're right," said Rose, picking up her purse.

"Good luck," Juanita said. "We'll leave you now." She followed Rose out of the room.

In the hallway, Rose turned to her. "It's such an exciting time. Hank and I hardly made it to his grandson Joshua's recent birth. And little Leah was almost as excited about her brother's birth as we were."

"Births and weddings. Two such wonderful times," said Juanita, leading Rose to her car.

Juanita dropped Rose off at her house and drove home. The past year had been sad with Alec's passing, but now life was beginning to regenerate. It felt good.

And later, when she received a phone call from Brian telling her Alec Thurston Walden had arrived healthy and with lusty cries, Juanita held Pedro's hand and cried tears of joy.

CHAPTER THIRTEEN
JUANITA

The next morning, as soon as Juanita received the call from Lily asking her to come to the hospital to see baby Alec, she called Ivy to tell her she'd be late to work and why. Then she hurried to her car, carrying the special package she'd kept for just this moment.

When she walked into the hospital room and saw Lily holding the baby, sentimental tears blurred her vision. Lily and Brian had decided to name their little boy after Alec. Now, staring at the little newborn as she drew closer, she was filled with wonder. One life had ended, another was beginning.

"Oh, Juanita, I'm so glad you're here!" Lily exclaimed. "I couldn't wait any longer to show him to you." Lily unwrapped the baby's blanket and touched the baby's ten toes. Her voice wobbled. "He's perfect. And we think he looks like Brian."

"He's beautiful, *Cariña*," whispered Juanita in awe of the baby's alertness, the way he seemed to look right at her.

Lily wrapped him up. "Want to hold him?"

Juanita couldn't speak. She simply held out her arms.

With the baby nestled against her, Juanita smiled as he closed his eyes. She couldn't wait for grandchildren, but in the meantime, she'd enjoy this little boy and his brother and sister. And Benjy, of course. She and Pedro had wanted more children, but that hadn't happened.

"Alec weighs 7 pounds, 1 ounce and is twenty inches long," Lily said proudly. "The nurses told me I did a great job, that first babies don't normally come this fast." She sighed. "I'm glad it's over."

Juanita kissed her cheek. "You did very well. I'm proud of you. But having the baby is only the beginning. But you'll do just fine."

Unexpected tears rolled down Lily's cheeks. "You have no idea what your words mean to me. I've been thinking about my mother. I don't want to be anything like her."

Juanita clasped her hand. "No worries. You've told me about her, and you're nothing like that. You've already proven what a good mother you are with Izzy and Ollie. This little one is coming into a good life with you." She handed Lily a tissue from the box next to her bed.

Lily wiped her eyes. "I'm sorry I'm so emotional."

"Don't worry, my darling, tears can sometimes be very healing." Juanita handed her the small, beribboned box she'd brought with her. "This is something Alec gave me, but I want you to have this. To keep for the baby."

Lily opened the box, and from the black velvet lining, she lifted a gold signet ring with an ornate initial A on the surface. "Oh, Juanita, I've seen Alec wear this. Are you sure you want to part with it?"

"I think it's only right that baby Alec have this. I just had a feeling that one of you Flowers would need this one day, and when I learned you and Brian were going to name the baby after Alec, I knew this should go to you."

"Oh-h-h, thanks so much, I promise to treasure it until the day we can give it to him," said Lily, taking the baby from her and settling him next to her on the pillow. She let out a trembling sigh. "I'm so happy I answered Alec's letter asking for my help. It's changed everything for me. Having you and Pedro, along with Rose and Willow, in my life, has made all the difference. I love you, Juanita."

"Love you too," said Juanita.

They turned as Willow and Rose entered the room together.

"Hi! Come see baby Alec! And the gift Juanita gave me," called Lily.

Amid the cooing from Willow and Rose over both the baby and the gift, Juanita took pictures on her phone and then kissed Lily. "I have to go to the Kitchen. See you later."

Juanita said goodbye to the others and left the room filled with emotion. The circle of life was as continual as the rising of the sun.

At the Kitchen, Juanita proudly showed everyone pictures of Lily and the baby. Even Isaac, as the only man, seemed thrilled to see them.

Soon all of Juanita's energy was focused on the work of getting ready for another day of serving a meal to the growing number of people arriving for a hot lunch.

The day went smoothly. One guest dropped his tray, but the mess was easily cleaned up. Juanita recognized more of the regulars and was glad to see that they, accustomed to the routine, moved quickly through the line being served.

Later, she waved goodbye to Ivy, who was leaving for school, and settled down with Benjy for an afternoon of reading and games.

There'd been only a few questions about Santa Claus from Benjy lately. She noticed that whenever Benjy saw Isaac, he stared at Isaac's round stomach and patted his own. Hiding her amusement, she figured he was remembering what Isaac had told him about Santa Claus being inside everyone. Pedro had told her that when he wasn't helping in the wood shop, Benjy was busy coloring special pictures for everyone. It amazed her that for Benjy this might be the first time he had a circle of people around him who were as close to a family as he'd ever had.

Her thoughts flew to Ivy. What must it have been like to have a baby at such a young age and then not have any support from her parents? The thought of it hurt.

CHAPTER FOURTEEN
IVY

Ivy studied the photos of Lily and the baby and felt memories of Benjy's birth weigh her down. Brushing them aside angrily, Ivy dug into work chopping, mixing, and supervising others. She couldn't afford to get off track. She had plans to keep Benjy and herself from getting hurt. Her parents' refusal to acknowledge either of them was as painful, as sharp a slap across the face as anything she could think of. Her parents' behavior both before and after Benjy's birth left scars she wasn't sure would ever heal. But she wouldn't let them ruin her.

The work at the Kitchen was a perfect situation for Benjy and her. Here, people were kind and appreciative. Juanita, especially, was like a haven of safety with her obvious love of Benjy and respect for her. Ivy found the hard core inside of her softening but didn't know when she'd be ready to open herself more.

Classes were over for the holidays at school, but Ivy still took time a couple of days a week to go to the college library to do research and to prep for next semester's classes. It was a time when she could be alone to gather her thoughts.

When Jake found her at the library one afternoon, rather than being annoyed, she was pleased to see him. They'd acknowledged each other at the Kitchen with smiles but she was always too busy to chat.

"I thought I might find you here." Jake plopped down on a chair beside her. "What are you doing for Christmas?"

"Ah've been invited to Willow's wedding. Lucita has promised to watch Benjy."

"Really? I'm going to the wedding too." He chuckled. "As Maribelle's date."

She laughed with him. Everyone loved Maribelle and were touched to see the two of them together.

"What about Christmas morning?" he asked quietly. "What are you doing then?"

She'd heard the wistfulness in his voice. "Ah'll be with Benjy, of course." She hesitated, and then added, "Would you like to come for breakfast? We don't celebrate Christmas, but Ah always make something special to eat."

"You sure?" Jake asked, his face lighting up. "I don't want to intrude."

"Ah'm sure." Ivy reached out and almost touched his hand before pulling away. "Ah know what it's like to be alone."

"Thanks. Sounds good."

"How'd you do on your exams?" Ivy asked.

A flush of color entered Jake's cheeks. "Couple Bs and an A. How about you?"

"Same," she said proudly.

"I'm serious about maybe working together in the future. Think about it." He rose to his feet. "Gotta go. I have to get back to Maribelle. She's having her hair done. Something new for the wedding, she told me."

Ivy returned his grin, trying to imagine Maribelle's new 'do. She was a most interesting woman, that's for sure.

CHAPTER FIFTEEN
JUANITA

The next day, when Juanita saw Maribelle's bright-purple hair, she grinned. On other people it might look foolish, but the new hairdo somehow fit the colorful woman with the irrepressible spirit.

"Good afternoon," she said to Maribelle as Jake led her inside the Kitchen. "How pretty you look."

Maribelle posed with one foot forward and an arm raised in the air. "I wanted to do something special for the wedding. It's all I can think about. Willow is going to make such a beautiful bride, and her beau reminds me an awful lot of Henry."

"We have some exciting news here at the Kitchen. Lily's baby arrived. A beautiful boy. I've got pictures. I'll show you later after the crowd goes."

Maribelle had become in the habit of staying late, sometimes long after she'd eaten. Juanita and the others didn't mind. She was like a tropical island in the sea of people around her. Most of the staff at one time or another found a chance to talk to her. Maribelle sometimes brought old photographs with her, a fascinating addition to her stories.

With school out for the Christmas holidays, Jake often brought Maribelle to the Kitchen and then sat and talked to some of the younger men who were appearing for the free food. Juanita suspected some were students like Jake, struggling to find a way to pay to go to school. She was also aware that Jake never missed a chance to say hi to Ivy.

Juanita gazed around at the crowd. It was an odd, diverse group of people who filled their dining room. Over time she learned some of the stories behind a number of the regular guests. They were mostly sad tales of lives gone wrong. Seeing them at the Kitchen, Juanita hoped a tasty hot meal might bring changes to them.

With the arrival of December 23rd, excitement among the staff grew. They'd been asked to return to the Kitchen at five for a holiday party Juanita and the Flowers had planned for them. Lucita's grandchildren, Ricardo and Eva, six and nine respectively, and Rosita's children—teenagers, Elsa and Elena, and little two-year-old Paco were invited to the party as well.

As preparations got under way, no one was more excited than Benjy.

Rose turned on Christmas music and the sound of joyous carols filled the space. Benjy raced from the kitchen to the door to greet every new arrival. Wearing a new red sweater Juanita had given him, he eagerly handed each child an iced Christmas cookie made the night before.

"Mama and Ah made this for you!" he proudly declared.

As the children entered the room, Juanita watched their eyes light up at seeing the packages beneath the Christmas tree. She'd had to explain to Benjy that these gifts were part of the real spirit of Christmas, that each one had been carefully chosen to suit the person receiving it with no thought of anything in return.

After everyone had arrived and were busy talking to one another, Benjy came over to Juanita and took hold of her hand. "Ah lak Chrissmus awready."

"Me too," said Juanita, giving his hand a squeeze of

affection. The buzz of conversation, the excited chatter of children pleased her.

Wearing a Santa hat, Rose tapped a spoon against a glass to get everyone's attention. "All right. Dinner will be served shortly. I've ordered some special food to be brought in for all of us. No work for our wonderful staff on this your special day."

"Merry Christmas and thank you to all of you," said Willow. "We're so happy we can be together for a little bit this evening."

Benjy stared at the Santa hat perched on top of Willow's head and tugged on Juanita's hand. "Are Ms. Willow and Ms. Rose supposed to be Santa Claus? Or are they elves, lak Ah think?"

"In a way, they're both," Juanita said, smiling down at him. "It looks like they're ready. Let's go get something to eat."

Two long tables had been pushed together to form a small buffet covered with a red cloth. In the center, a collection of battery candles flickered in red glass holders sitting on a mirror, adding a brightness to the table and display of food.

A small ham sat at one end of the table, a turkey breast at the other end. In between, casseroles, salads, rolls, and fixings for sandwiches filled the space. Rose served the ham to those who wanted it; Willow helped others to turkey.

It did Juanita's heart good to see the staff being served. They worked hard and deserved this show of gratitude.

She helped Rosita and Lucita make sure the kids got what they needed. She looked down at Benjy's plate—sliced turkey, mashed potatoes, gravy, and three green beans.

"Good job except for veggies," she said.

He shook his head. "Ah just don't lak those bee-eens."

Juanita chuckled. "Well, then, you only have to eat three."

She turned as little Ricardo approached carrying a plate of

food. A handsome boy of six, he and Benjy sometimes played together. "*Gracias, Doña Sanchez.*"

"*De nada, Ricardo,*" Juanita said. *Such good manners.* His grandmother, Lucita, was doing a good job raising him and his sister. She wondered if their mother would show up tomorrow. Probably not. Lucita had told her that her daughter didn't come home very often. And when she did, she was usually high on something and wanting money.

As Juanita talked to members of the staff and their children, she realized respect and kindness had turned to much more —she loved them like family.

She gazed across the room at Rose and Willow laughing and chatting as they stayed at the buffet making sure everyone had their fill of the food.

Leaving them to their jobs, she took a seat at one of the tables next to Natasha. "This must always seem a special time of year for you."

"You mean with my name meaning Christmas?" Natasha said, smiling. "Some years have been better than others. This one is very special thanks to you and the other women. Is Lily going to be able to attend?"

"She promised to drop by. She wants everyone to see the baby. And Izzy and Ollie are excited about the party."

As if her words had prompted it, Lily appeared at the front door with the baby and her older kids.

"Hi, everyone!" Lily said, coming inside and closing the door behind her. "I can't stay long, but I wanted everyone to be able to meet Alec." Izzy pouted at Lily's side.

Juanita hurried over to Izzy and hugged her close. At four, she was understandably a little jealous of the baby. "How's the big sister doing?"

"Daddy says I'm not the baby anymore. I'm his big girl," said Izzy, glancing slant-wise at the baby.

"You're also the only girl in the family. That's very special," said Juanita. She turned to Ollie. "And how's the big brother?"

"Tired," he said with his straightforward manner. "The baby has things mixed up. He sleeps during the day and is awake at night. It's exhausting."

"Oh, my! That's not easy on anyone. Well, you'd better come and get some food," said Juanita, amused by the interchange.

Rose and Willow left Lily's side and hurried to help Juanita serve Lily's kids.

Lily proudly displayed little Alec to everyone and then said, "It's his feeding time. I'll be back as soon as I can." She left with the baby, and the excitement over seeing him died down, leaving the room filled with a quieter buzz.

When Rose brought out dessert on a rolling cart, the kids all got up from their seats to get a closer look at the cake shaped like a snowman. Covered in white icing, the body of the snowman, Juanita knew, contained chocolate cake. The big round head was full of white cake.

A circle formed around the treat. The kids watched carefully as Rose sliced the cake apart, carefully following requests for different flavors. When the younger set had their choice of cake, Juanita and Willow handed out slices to the adults.

"Anyone want ice cream?" Willow asked.

Several hands went up.

While Willow was busy taking care of that, Lily returned and greeted everyone.

Juanita took orders for coffee and spent several minutes getting it ready.

"You should sit," Ivy said to Juanita. "I'll pass out coffee for everyone."

"No, sweetheart, it's our time to show you and the other

staff members how much we appreciate your help."

Ivy studied her with a look of surprise, nodded, and sat down. "Thanks."

After the cake was mostly eaten, the children started to get restless, Rose called everyone to order. "Time for presents." She waved Isaac over to her and placed her Santa hat on top of his balding head. "Isaac is going to hand them out."

Grinning with pride, Isaac walked over to the chair set up by the tree and sat down.

"Ho! Ho! Ho! Anyone here who doesn't like Christmas?" he said, beaming at the children who'd quickly formed a group sitting on the floor in front of him.

He raised a finger in front of him. "I've been told that each one of you wanted one special gift. Let's see if there's something here for you. Wait until everyone else has their gift, then you can open yours."

Isaac seemed as excited as the child whose name he called, handing their gift to them and then clapping, causing the others in the room to clap too.

Juanita kept an eye on Benjy as one name and then another was called. When it came down to the last gift, Benjy glanced at her with a look of worry.

"Benjy! Come get your gift!" cried Isaac, breaking into that moment.

Grinning, Benjy raced over to him and hugged the wrapped box to him.

"Okay, kids, now you can open your gifts."

Amid the sound of paper being ripped and cries of excitement, Juanita watched as Benjy set his gift down on the floor beside him but did nothing to open it.

She came and knelt beside him. "Aren't you going to open it?"

He shook his head. "Nope. I'm saving it for Christmas Day,

cause it's all I'm gonna git."

"Now why would you say that?" Juanita suspected she knew the answer but had to ask.

He glanced at Ivy and whispered in Juanita's ear. "Mama doesn't believe. Not yet. But she will."

"Really? How?"

"You'll see." Benjy gave her a triumphant smile. "Papa Pedro and Ah have it all figured out."

"Okay then. Do you want to put your gift back under the tree so it's here for you on Christmas?"

Benjy nodded. "That way Ah can pretend it's from Santa."

Juanita sighed, wondering what past Christmases must have been like for this precious little boy.

Before everyone left promptly at seven, envelopes with bonuses were handed out to all the staff members.

After saying goodbye to everyone, Ivy climbed the stairs with Benjy. "I'll see you tomorrow. We're going to stay upstairs for the rest of the night. Thank you again for everything. It was wonderful."

Benjy raced over to Juanita and threw his arms around her waist. Looking up at her, he grinned. "Shh. Don't say anything to Mama about her surprise."

"I won't. I promise." She gave him an extra hug.

"Come along, Benjy. Everyone is tired," said Ivy. "Are you sure Ah can't help with the cleanup?"

"It's all been taken care of," said Rose. "The caterers have done most of it. We'll see that the rest is done and lock up behind ourselves."

"Okay, thanks." Ivy waved and took Benjy's elbow, and they walked up the stairs.

"How about a glass of wine?" said Willow as Juanita walked into the kitchen. Rose and Lily were wiping down counters. "I tucked a bottle inside my purse. Thought it would be nice to celebrate Juanita's Kitchen's first Christmas party."

"Great idea," said Rose. "I wish we could've offered everyone wine, but without a license, we couldn't take the chance. Should I get glasses?"

"No," said Willow. "I've brought proper wine glasses too."

Juanita chuckled. "Alec taught you well, my daughter."

Willow's eyes gleamed. "He taught me about good wine too. We have a lovely pinot noir from the Willamette Valley tonight. A Chandler Hill wine."

"As Benjy would say, that's lak music to my eahs," said Rose.

They laughed together.

CHAPTER SIXTEEN
JUANITA

Juanita lay in bed thinking about the day ahead. She'd go into the Kitchen to make sure staff and volunteers showed up and then she'd have the rest of the day to begin preparing for the rehearsal dinner tonight and Willow's wedding tomorrow. Willow had arranged for her and the two other Flowers to join her for an afternoon of pampering at a local spa. She'd also bribed a hair salon into handling them Christmas morning in return for a one-night stay at the Premio Inn in January.

She checked the clock and rolled out of bed. Pedro was already up. The smell of fresh coffee wafted to her from the kitchen. After years of getting up early to do yard work for Alec, Pedro still wasn't able to sleep in.

When Juanita walked into the kitchen, Pedro was sitting at the table with a stack of drawings in front of him.

"What are you doing?" she asked, grabbing a cup of coffee and going to his side.

"You have to see these." He held up one of the drawings. "Benjy drew a picture for every staff member in the kitchen. Seems Isaac told him Santa—the spirit of giving—is in all of us, and he took it to heart."

Juanita took one of the drawings in her hands and studied the picture Benjy had drawn of Isaac. A large, round-bellied, dark-skinned man stared back at her with a wide smile and a Santa hat on top of his head. In his hand, he held a cake. *I love you* was printed at the bottom.

Tears stung Juanita's eyes. Isaac had been appointed to baking in the kitchen, and they'd discovered he had a real knack for making cakes. She suspected his gentle nature encouraged the cakes to be extra light and fluffy.

Pedro handed her the rest.

In each picture, the figure wore a Santa hat, and Benjy had written the words "*I love you*" at the bottom. But each drawing was different, showing a unique side of each person.

Lucita had gray hair and musical notes coming from her mouth. Juanita smiled. Lucita loved to sing as they worked, her strong, sweet voice rising in the air to please them all.

Juanita looked at the others. Rosita stood with two girls and a small boy, Summer had flowing yellow hair and big blue eyes, and Natasha had what Juanita thought was a scarf around her throat. Something she often wore.

"Where's one of Ivy?" Juanita asked.

Pedro reached over and carefully lifted a picture with a lot of glittering sprinkles glued to a drawing of a Christmas tree with two packages beside it. Next to the tree stood a woman with a halo above her head. Wings spread from behind her back. Beside her was a boy wearing a Santa hat and holding a big red heart.

"Oh, my!" gasped Juanita, taking a seat. She clasped a hand to her heart. "This drawing says so much!" She felt the prickle of tears and waved a hand in front of her face to settle her emotions. "It makes me wonder what the two of them have been through. In so many ways, Benjy is wise beyond his years."

"In other ways, he's just a little boy who wants a Christmas like his classmates," said Pedro. "But he really likes the idea of giving to others. Once I explained what Isaac meant when he said we all have Santa—the spirit of giving—inside us, Benjy understood."

"Why do you have his drawings?" said Juanita.

"I promised to deliver them to him at the Kitchen this afternoon so he can hand them out before the staff leaves. It's a surprise he's planned for them."

"I love that boy," said Juanita. "He's making this holiday so special." She reached over and clasped Pedro's hand. "And so is Willow. She's always wanted a Christmas wedding. It's hard to believe the time has come, but it's going to be beautiful."

"I don't know if I'm ready," said Pedro, shaking his head. "It's a whole new phase for the two of us."

"We've made it this far; we can do this, the two of us together," said Juanita. She couldn't hold back a smile. "In fact, I was thinking after Juanita's Kitchen settles into a more comfortable routine, we could begin to do some traveling. You've talked about seeing all the states. We could get an RV like you once talked about."

Pedro's face brightened. "Really? You'd do that for me? That could be something we give to one another."

Juanita was still smiling. "Sounds like a plan to me." Suddenly the prospect of the two of them alone seemed a wonderful adventure.

When she went into the Kitchen, everything was running smoothly. The staff, knowing they'd have Christmas off seemed to be making a special effort to make the day a good one for all.

Juanita was pleased that a couple of churches in the area were holding their annual Christmas Dinner for people in the area, and the burden could be lifted from Juanita's Kitchen. The break it provided to them was especially appreciated during this, their first month in operation.

When she left the Kitchen shortly after two, she was more

than ready for a spa treatment. That, and simply enjoying some time with the three Flowers. Each woman was so different, with intriguing backgrounds and bright futures, that spending time with them always made her feel exhilarated.

Willow and the others met her at a place simply called The Spa.

"After a massage or a facial, whichever you choose, we are all going to share a light tea in the garden room," said Willow, giving her a kiss hello. "We don't want to eat too much before dinner at Tico's. Craig has requested a roasted pig for the occasion."

Juanita's mouth watered. She loved *lechón*. "How nice!"

"He's much happier that we're doing something less formal than we'd first planned." Willow said. "I think he should have the rehearsal dinner however he wishes because my wedding day is planned just the way I want it. Including having you all be a part of it." She turned to Juanita. "One other change. I've invited Benjy to the wedding. He was so curious about all the details I thought he should have a chance to see for himself. Ivy agreed."

Juanita looked at the sweet, lovely young woman who was her daughter and wondered how she could be so lucky.

Later, feeling thoroughly relaxed following her massage, Juanita sat at a glass-topped table drinking water with lemon and eating small tea sandwiches filled with cream cheese and cucumbers, salmon, egg salad with capers, and other combinations of light fare.

She wondered how Pedro had done delivering the drawings for Benjy and sent a quick text asking him. One quickly came back: *Here now.*

CHAPTER SEVENTEEN
IVY

When Ivy saw Pedro arrive just before closing, she was surprised but pleased. He was a sweet man who'd spent quite a bit of time with Benjy doing various craft projects.

"Hello, Ivy. I'm here for Benjy."

Before she could call for him, Benjy came rushing down the stairway. "Hi, Papa Pedro! Do you have them?"

Pedro stood by the doorway. "Yes. Let me get them from the car. I'll be right back."

He returned shortly with a stack of papers in his hands.

Benjy took them and carried them proudly into the kitchen. "I've got something for you!" he announced.

Ivy shot Pedro a questioning look.

He smiled and winked at her.

Together, they watched Benjy hand out the drawings. The first to Isaac with a gentle pat to his stomach. The next to Lucita, then the others, one by one. When he got to the bottom one, he turned to her. "For you, Mama."

Ivy glanced at it, studied the details, emotion welling inside her. She tried, she really tried to stop any tears from forming, tried to stop them from rolling down her cheeks. When she realized she couldn't, for one of those rare moments in her life, she let them flow.

"You don't like it?" Benjy said, giving her a worried look.

"I *love* it," she said, kneeling on the floor and drawing him to her. Normally, she wouldn't allow anyone to see her in such a vulnerable state, but she'd noticed the kitchen staff fighting tears of their own.

As she hugged Benjy to her, Ivy knew she had to see things differently. It had taken her darling son and their new, odd family of sorts to make her understand.

CHAPTER EIGHTEEN

JUANITA

Wearing a bright turquoise dress that brought a look of admiration from Pedro, Juanita entered Tico's with him, ready to begin the joyous celebration of Willow's and Craig's next-day wedding.

Watching the two of them talking to Craig's father and Loretta and Ricardo Morales, she thought how very lucky they all were with this union. It pleased her also that the rehearsal dinner was in a setting that gave a nod to Willow's background. It seemed only right.

Willow came over to her. "Mom, you look gorgeous!" She turned to Pedro and gave him a hug. "Come join the rest! We're ready to party!"

Juanita followed Willow over to where a group was standing at one end of the room in front of a bartender taking orders for drinks. Though she didn't normally drink much, she ordered a margarita. Tonight, was a once-in-a-lifetime celebration.

Mariachi music played in the background as she greeted Loretta. They'd known and liked one another from church and enjoyed time together when the men got together to play golf or to watch sports. But now, with Craig marrying Willow, the bond between the two women was even closer.

Rose and Lily arrived with their spouses, along with Sarah Jensen and her husband, Eric, now an ex-military man. She hadn't spent much time with Eric, but she liked him. Craig had chosen him to be in the wedding party along with Hank and

Brian, to keep things simple and within the Desert Sage Inn family.

What began as a pleasant evening turned into a sentimental journey about the families and how they'd all interacted with Alec.

At one point, the trio who sang at the restaurant on a regular basis came into the room and entertained them. Listening to the sounds of guitars and the harmonizing of their music, including *Bésame Mucho,* Juanita sighed with satisfaction. It was a lovely beginning to Willow and Craig's celebration.

After the last bit of food had been eaten, the last toast given, Pedro turned to her. "I think it's safe to go now. Ivy and Benjy should be sound asleep at this late hour."

All eyes turned to them as they rose.

"Time to go?" Willow said.

Pedro nodded. "We have a special errand to do."

Hugs and kisses were exchanged, and then Juanita and Pedro climbed into their car and headed off for their very special mission.

Pedro pulled into the entrance to the parking lot of Juanita's Kitchen and stopped the car there rather than get any closer. He turned the car facing out for a quick getaway.

Feeling excitement pulse through her, Juanita got out of the car and waited for Pedro to lift the cloth sack from the back seat. He'd made a pact with Benjy to hide a present for his mother by the tree.

Quietly, Juanita and Pedro made their way to the entrance of the building. Juanita silently unlocked the door, checked for any sign of life, and waved her partner in this Christmas caper inside. All was dark, with only the light from outside streetlamps to guide them.

Juanita stifled a giggle at the sight of Pedro on tiptoes making his way stealthily across the darkened room. With the sack in his hand, he looked like a fledgling burglar.

She followed him and huddled by the tree, ready to accept the packages he handed to her. The tree was wide and thick enough that they could easily tuck several packages behind it.

The gift for Ivy would be placed in front as Benjy had instructed Pedro.

At the sound of the icemaker in the kitchen, Juanita froze. Nobody stirred. Holding her breath, she put the last of the packages behind the tree and stood.

Her pulse racing and feeling every nerve ending awake with caution, Juanita quietly crossed the room behind Pedro and slipped outside. Careful not to make a sound, she locked the door, and then walked quickly across the parking lot to where Pedro waited for her.

She slipped inside the car and studied the building. There was no movement.

Juanita took her first deep breath as Pedro eased out of the parking lot.

"That's the most Christmas fun I've had in years," she said, turning to him. "Let's hope it works."

Pedro winked at her. "Everyone needs a little Christmas magic."

CHAPTER NINETEEN
IVY

Ivy felt a hand on her shoulder and startled, came wide awake. Groaning, she checked the bedside clock. Six a.m.

"Wake up! Santa's been here," said Benjy, his voice breathless with excitement. "Ah saw a gift for you near the tree."

"Wha-a-t? How long have you been awake?" Ivy murmured, rubbing her eyes and trying to focus on Benjy's shining face.

He tugged on her hand. "C'mon! We have to go see! Ah know it's for you."

She placed her feet on the floor, grabbed the flannel robe she always used, wrapped it around her, and did her best to keep up with Benjy as he ran down the stairs.

"See?" said Benjy, pointing to a box wrapped in silver paper with a white bow on top.

She blinked. Sure enough, Benjy's gift from the party and another silvery package sat on the floor together in front of the tree.

"How'd that get here?" Ivy asked, studying Benjy's face. His eyes were alight with excitement, his smile bright and wide.

"It was Santa Claus. Ah just know it."

She allowed him to drag her closer, and when she bent over to study it, the name "Ivy" was clearly printed out on the gift card.

"You've got to open it, Mama," Benjy said, handing it to her.

She held the present close to her, wondering why she'd ever thought of sharing her parents' grim belief about the holidays.

"Go ahead. Ah can't wait any longer," said Benjy dancing on his toes with excitement.

She carefully removed the shiny silver wrapping and opened the plain cardboard box. Inside, tissue hid what was beneath. She pushed it aside and stared at the beautiful wooden box inside. Her name was carved into the wood across the top of it.

"Do you lak it?" Benjy asked.

Ivy rubbed her fingers across the wood, marveling at its smoothness. "It's beautiful. Did you make it?"

Benjy shook his head. "No, and neither did Papa Pedro. This is from Santa Claus."

"Ah see," she said softly. "And how did he know my name?"

"Because Santa Claus knows things lak that," Benjy said. "He's everywhere. Inside of all of us."

Ivy sat down on the floor and pulled Benjy onto her lap. "He's certainly inside of you. Thank you, Benjy and Santa, for such a beautiful, thoughtful gift. Now, why don't you open your gift from the party. It's time."

Benjy reached over and drew the box to him. Ripping the paper off with joyful abandon, he shouted, "Yay! Ah wanted this game player!!" He turned to her round-eyed. "Who's this from?"

"Read the tag," Ivy said. "Ah believe it says Santa Claus." She got up and went to plug in the Christmas tree lights and stopped in shock. "Benjy! Come here! Look what Ah found!"

Benjy raced to her side. "What? Where'd they come from?"

"Ah don't know," said Ivy. "Seems like something magical is going on. Help me get them out of there."

Ivy handed him a dozen wrapped gifts of different sizes. She plugged in the lights and turned to face him.

He gazed at her, his eyes round. "Do you think these are really from Santa?"

Ivy paused. She'd always been totally honest with him. "If, like you say, Santa is in all of us, then Ah say yes. These must be from Santa Claus." No use telling him that in this case, she suspected Santa Claus might be in the form of two of the loveliest people she'd ever met, a couple she wished were her parents.

She watched as Benjy carefully read the name tags and put the packages into two different piles.

Later, after they'd opened each gift carefully, taking their time to admire each one, Ivy knew that no matter what the future years held, she'd always remember this, their first real Christmas together.

CHAPTER TWENTY
JUANITA

Juanita rolled over in bed and faced Pedro. "Merry Christmas!" she whispered in his ear as she nestled closer to him.

He opened his eyes and smiled before kissing her.

A warm tingle swept through her, the kind she'd told Willow to wait for when choosing a man to marry.

When they pulled apart, Pedro said, "Wait here. I have something for you."

He returned, carrying a wrapped package, and handed it to her. "It's something special. You'll see why."

Juanita unwrapped the gift and gasped softly at the sight of a beautiful, wooden box he'd made himself. The polished wood was smooth against her fingers. Her name was carved along the top of it.

"Benjy and I spent hours sanding it between coats of finish," Pedro said with pride.

"It's gorgeous," said Juanita. "I love that the two of you made it together."

"Open it up," Pedro said.

She lifted the lid and froze. Against the black velvet lining a diamond pendant and necklace sparkled up at her. Her vision became unclear through the sheen of tears.

"*Cariña, te amo,*" Pedro said, bending to kiss her. "I wanted you to have this for our daughter's wedding, for the beautiful mother you are."

Juanita lifted the solitaire diamond on a delicate white-gold chain and let out a trembling breath. "It's perfect."

"Let me help you with it," Pedro said. He took it from her and hooked it around her neck. "There. It's almost as beautiful as you are."

Juanita smiled up into his eyes. They'd worked hard all their lives, had done without some things as they scrimped and saved for Willow's future, but Pedro had always found the right words to make her believe how rich her life was with him.

Later that morning, as Juanita entered the beauty salon where she was to meet the Flowers, she arranged her new necklace carefully atop her sweater. She was proud of it and couldn't wait for them to see it.

Henri, Therese, and Bianca, dressed in their usual work clothes, greeted her with cries of "Welcome to The Spa! Merry Christmas!" and "Happy Wedding Day!"

Juanita looked around. "Thank you so much for helping us out today. Where are the others?"

"In the back room," said Henri. "Come this way."

Juanita followed him into a room that normally served as the nail salon. Willow came over to her. "You're here! Join us for a little wedding day mimosa!"

Willow caught sight of the necklace and beamed. "Oh, it looks perfect on you! I helped *Papi* pick it out. Don't you love it!"

Rose and Lily crowded around them.

"Oh, Juanita! It's beautiful!" cried Lily.

"We've been so excited for you," Rose said.

"You knew about it all this time?" Juanita said, chuckling.

"Willow couldn't wait to tell us," said Lily. "Such a special gift for such a special woman." She lifted her glass of water. "Hope you don't mind, but Henri's going to work on me first so I can get home to the kids."

"How's it going?" Juanita noted the circles under Lily's eyes and remembered how difficult the early days with newborns were. Apparently, little Alec wasn't the angel he appeared to be.

"The baby is starting to sleep a bit longer during the night, but he's still a little mixed up. The good thing is both Izzy and Ollie aren't complaining about having quiet time in the afternoon. Bless their hearts, they often end up napping." She laughed. "After getting up at five o'clock this morning to open gifts, I believe we'll all be napping this afternoon before the wedding."

Juanita hugged her. "You're doing a good job, Lily." She knew how important those words were to her.

Lily hugged her back, then at Henri's signal, she went with him to the front room.

"Here's to the mother of the bride." Willow handed her a glass with orange juice and champagne. "Thank you for everything!" Though Willow had shouldered most of the expense of the wedding, Juanita and Pedro had insisted, over Willow's objections, to pay for the wedding dress and half of the reception.

"It's such a special day," Juanita said. "I'm so happy for you, my darling."

Willow's smile was tender. "I know you've been feeling a little blue with all the recent changes, maybe you and *Papi* should make some plans of your own."

"Funny you should say that," said Juanita with a note of excitement she couldn't hide. "Your father and I have decided to buy an RV and travel around the country."

Willow's look of astonishment changed into laugher. "I should've known you'd figure it out on your own. After helping Alec all those years, you both deserve to have some fun on your own."

Juanita raised her glass in a toast. "I second that."

"What are you toasting?" asked Rose, coming to stand by them.

"Mom and Dad are buying an RV and are planning to do some traveling."

"Fabulous," said Rose. "Don't you worry about Juanita's Kitchen. Our whole purpose was to be able to work on getting it set up together and then training someone else to run it for us."

The idea of seeing the future as a new beginning made Juanita's pulse quicken.

CHAPTER TWENTY-ONE
IVY

After opening gifts with Benjy, Ivy went into the kitchen to whip up her favorite cranberry muffins. She'd invited Jake for a special Christmas breakfast, and she didn't want to disappoint him.

While the muffins were baking, she ran upstairs to quickly shower and dress. Benjy was in his bedroom looking at the new pants and shirt she'd bought him for the wedding.

"Ah know you're proud of them, but don't put on those clothes yet. This morning, dress in your regular clothes. It's just Jake coming for breakfast."

"Jake's your friend from school?"

"Yes, a very nice man who wants to open a business with me someday. We'll see."

Benjy studied her. "Do you lak him?"

"Sure. Lak Ah said, he's a nice man."

Benjy caught the corner of his lip and nodded. "Okay."

Not long after that, Jake arrived carrying a brown paper bag and bringing a puff of fresh, cold air with him into the building. "Mm-m-m. Something smells good! Merry Christmas!" He held up a large brown paper bag. "I brought some goodies. 'Thought you might like to try my special mimosa. I make it with a dry, bubbling wine from Spain."

"That sounds good," said Ivy. She put her arm around Benjy. "Jake, I should introduce you formally. This is my son Benjy. He and Ah are a strong team."

Jake squatted in front of Benjy. "I've heard a lot of good

things about you from your Mom. Did she tell you that I want her to come to work with me someday?"

Benjy nodded his head solemnly. "Raht now, she works at the Kitchen."

"Oh, yes. I wouldn't want to interfere with that. She's doing important work here." Jake looked up at her and smiled.

Ivy felt her cheeks flush with pleasure and quickly turned away.

Jake followed her into the kitchen, set down the bag he was carrying on the kitchen counter, and faced Benjy. "I brought you a gift." He handed him a small box wrapped in red paper.

Benjy's eyes lit up. "For me?"

"Yeah. It's pretty cool. I used to like to do stuff like this when I was younger."

Benjy unwrapped the box of Legos every child loves and cried, "Oh, wow! Thank you!" He turned to Ivy. "See what Ah mean about Santa?"

Ivy chuckled. "Yes, everyone is proving that to me today."

While Benjy took the box over to the rug beside the kitchen table and emptied the pieces there, she watched as Jake pulled two tall wine glasses, a bottle of wine, and a carton of orange juice from the bag.

"I want you to tell me if you think this mimosa is as good as I think it is. It would be a staple in the catering business."

Hearing him talk about it, Ivy wondered what it would be like to go into business with him one day. He was very serious about it, and she already knew what a hard worker he was. Ambitious too. All good points.

He smiled at her as he handed her the drink he'd measured carefully. Lifting his own glass, he clinked it against hers. "Thank you for inviting me here. It's the nicest Christmas I've had in a long time."

He bent down and kissed her on the cheek before she could

even think to protest.

Feeling the heat from his lips on her skin, she took a swallow of the drink to cool herself. She'd dated occasionally but shut things down before it could go anywhere. Now, she liked the idea of getting to know Jake better.

Later, as she prepared an omelet, with Jake observing her every move, she drew on her past experiences working in a variety of kitchens to make it light and fluffy. And when Jake declared the breakfast the best he'd ever eaten, she filled with pride.

While she cleaned up, Jake settled on the floor beside Benjy. She watched as they worked together to complete the space ship from a design the kit had provided. Seeing them like this, she wondered what it would be like if their relationship went forward.

When it was time for him to leave, she walked him to the door slowly. He'd filled the kitchen with a personal warmth she'd enjoyed, and from the look on Benjy's face, he was as smitten as she.

"I'll be back to pick you up for the wedding. 'Sure you don't mind riding in Maribelle's old car?"

She laughed. "Ah don't want to disappoint Maribelle. She's talking about making a big entrance at the hotel."

Jake shook his head and smiled. "She makes a big entrance no matter where she goes."

Ivy waved goodbye, shut the door, and leaned against it.

Benjy studied her. "Do you lak him, Mama? Really lak him?"

She studied his eager expression and ruffled his hair. "Ah believe Ah do."

CHAPTER TWENTY-TWO
JUANITA

Juanita checked the clock and rose from her bed where she'd been resting. The Flowers, as she thought of them, would be here soon to dress and get ready for the wedding. Earlier, Willow had brought over her dress, shoes, and makeup kit, along with the dresses Rose and Lily would be wearing. The dark green maternity outfit that Lily had chosen to wear for the ceremony had been replaced by something a little more flattering in the same color.

The four o'clock ceremony was going to be held at the same church where Alec's memorial service had taken place. It was a lovely location with a simple statement of belief in its décor.

She'd just freshened up when she heard the sound of voices coming from the living room. She hurried to greet Willow, Rose, and Lily.

As the Flowers took over her bedroom and bath, Juanita filled with excitement. Like so many of her friends had told her, a wedding was just what they all needed after months of tending to Alec. He would've loved to be part of this day because he thought of Willow as his own daughter. Life was funny, Juanita mused as she entered into the activity. What had started out as a way to help a new member of the family had created another one that grew from friendships.

She sat still as Rose applied light makeup to her face and smoothed eyeshadow across her eyelids before putting mascara on her lashes. She didn't normally wear a lot of makeup, but when she saw the effect in the mirror, she decided to do it more often. Her dark eyes seemed bigger and her cheeks more alive with a little blush.

"Mom, you look wonderful," gushed Willow.

Pleased, Juanita stood aside so Rose could do her magic on Willow.

She slid her red silk dress on and sighed with relief when she saw her image in the full-length mirror on her wall. It was as lovely as she remembered.

"Beautiful," murmured Lily, helping Juanita zip up her dress.

"You, too," said Juanita. Lily was very different from the shy, quiet woman who'd first showed up in Palm Desert to help Alec with the sale of his hotel. A confident woman now, secure with her husband's love and the dream of a family come true, Lily was still as sweet as ever.

Juanita gazed at Rose dressed in the dark shade of green that set off her red hair and matched the green in her eyes. Rose had seemed very self-assured when she'd returned to the desert to help Alec. In time, Juanita had learned that beneath that first impression, there was a lot more to Rose than she'd first thought. Tender, funny, caring, and vulnerable were just a few surprises that had emerged. Hank, her husband, was a perfect match for her. He adored her for all the ways she met the challenge of being a capable woman in a man's work world.

The last to get dressed, Willow slipped the white dress on and waited for help zipping it up and making sure all hooks were attended to.

When Juanita stepped away from Willow and stood beside her staring into the mirror, tears filled her eyes. "*Cariña. Eres tan hermosa.* You are so beautiful."

"*Gracias, Mami.*"

They smiled at one another.

In that smile, Juanita saw all the hopes and dreams she'd wished for her daughter come true.

"Willow, you're gorgeous!" said Rose.

"Simply stunning," added Lily, gathering around Willow.

A knock sounded at the door.

Juanita opened it and smiled when she noticed Pedro's eyes widen at the sight of their daughter.

"So beautiful," Juanita murmured.

He nodded, drew a deep breath, and let it out slowly. "Our little girl."

"Is it time to leave?" Juanita asked him.

"Yes, the limousines are here." He stood by holding the door as the women filed past them. And then he rushed ahead to help the drivers assist them into the cars.

The minister met them at a side door to the church and ushered them into a private room to wait for the guests to arrive. Willow and Craig had kept the number below one hundred, wanting it to be a small, intimate wedding with only family and close friends included.

Rose cracked open the door and seeing Hank, waved him over.

Standing behind Rose, Juanita admired him in his black tux, sprigs of mistletoe and holly pinned to his chest.

"Good luck, everyone!" Hank said after kissing Rose.

The door closed behind him and the harpist that had been hired continued playing musical notes that hung in the air with anticipation.

The florist came into the room with an assistant. Each had a large box in her hands.

"The corsage for the mother of the bride. The mother of the groom already has hers."

Juanita stood still while the corsage, a white orchid set off by a mixture of mistletoe and holly and wrapped with a green and red ribbon that matched her dress, was pinned to it.

Rose and Lily held up their bouquets. The same flowers made a beautiful nosegay, wrapped with the green and red ribbon.

"Gorgeous," said Juanita. She turned to look at the bouquet Willow was holding. Filled with white orchids accented with the dark green leaves of holly and the white berries of the mistletoe, it too was stunning in its simplicity.

Brian tapped on the door. "Time for me to walk you down the aisle, *Doña* Juanita."

Taking a deep breath, she kissed Willow, waved to the others, and left the room.

Walking slowly to accommodate Brian's prosthesis and her own steady but slow pace as she'd been instructed, Juanita took the opportunity to gaze at the audience. She saw a bright spot of purple and smiled at the back of Maribelle's head. Sitting on top of her purple hair was a hat made of purple netting. Beside her was Jake and to his right, Ivy sat with Benjy.

At the end of each pew, sprigs of mistletoe and holly hung wrapped in ribbon.

Friends and a few family members caught her attention, and she smiled at them all, happy for their presence.

She was seated in the front row, opposite the aisle from Loretta and Ricardo. Ken was standing at Craig's side as his son's best man.

Brian led Lily down the aisle. Seeing them together, Juanita smiled. She and Alec had thought they'd make a perfect pair.

Rose and Hank followed, looking at each other with such love, it made Juanita think of their wedding not long ago.

The harp music changed tempo with the sounds of a song Willow and Craig had chosen together for the processional. Juanita stood and turned to see Pedro leading Willow down the aisle. Juanita wasn't the only one who gasped softly at such a moment and dabbed at her eyes with a tissue. Willow was truly a dark-haired beauty as she walked forward with a look of joy on her face, her eyes holding a steady gaze on Craig.

In the murmuring that continued, Juanita heard Benjy. "Ms. Willow looks lak an angel, doesn't she, Mama?"

Juanita agreed. Willow looked exactly like one. Her dress, the one that had taken forever to find, fit her perfectly. Strapless with a beaded bodice and a white tulle overlay, it had three-quarter sleeves and a cowl neckline. At the waistline, a delicate woven band with a bow accented by holly and mistletoe brightened the dress as chiffon fell from it in soft layers to her feet. As Willow moved, the gorgeous material seemed to float around her.

She noticed the sheen in Craig's eyes and knew he, too, was in awe of his bride. Pedro kissed Willow and then handed her over to him. Craig leaned over and kissed her, unwilling to wait until the end of the ceremony.

Pedro sat beside Juanita, taking hold of her hand and squeezing it tightly with emotion.

Juanita drifted through the words remembering many moments in Willow's life, treasuring them all. And when she heard the vows Willow and Craig spoke to one another, so full of love and dedication, it seemed right that they both had waited for this moment to find true love.

"And now the groom may kiss the bride," the minister said.

Craig swept Willow into his arms and kissed her for so long, the minister cleared his throat.

Turning, still smiling, they faced the guests and then let out whoops of joy!

Laughing with the rest, Juanita waited behind for the photographer to take pictures. He'd filmed the service but had just a short while to capture the late-afternoon light in wedding photos before the sun would go down.

Loretta came over to her. "The ceremony was beautiful and so are you, *mi querida amiga.*"

Juanita hugged her. "I know, my dear friend, you've waited a long time for this moment."

"It was worth the wait." She and Juanita exchanged soft laughs. Craig had been a sought-after young man who hadn't been ready to settle down, even with Loretta's prompts.

After photographs and videos were taken, they headed to the hotel for the reception. By choosing to have it at Alec's former hotel, they hoped to feel his presence.

CHAPTER TWENTY-THREE
JUANITA

Juanita climbed into the stretch limousine with Pedro, Lily, Rose, and their spouses, eager to celebrate. It had been a beautiful wedding, living up to all her dreams. Best of all, it was a happy one, with the bride and groom obviously in love and committed to one another.

Willow and Craig were going to Hawaii for their honeymoon but would stay in a large suite at the hotel tonight.

When the limo pulled up in front of the Desert Sage Inn, Juanita was amused to see Maribelle's old classic car parked off to the side. Someday, it would be nice to see the car fixed up, but for now it served to carry the irrepressible woman who tended to live in the past when she'd been a star.

After Juanita was helped out of the car, she and Pedro entered the hotel and went directly to the private room where the buffet reception was being held.

At the doorway, Trace Armstrong greeted them. "Congratulations, Mr. and Mrs. Sanchez. I hope you find everything to your satisfaction."

"Thank you." Juanita smiled, but without her usual warmth. Trace Armstrong and his cousin, Brent Armstrong, had been rivals of Willow, determined to win a management position at this hotel. Willow had outdone them both by being appointed the actual manager of the Premio Inn after The Blaise Hotel Group had acquired it to complement their ownership of the Desert Sage Inn.

Pedro shook hands with Trace and they went inside. The

room had been decorated with sparkling lights, holiday greens, and flickering candles atop tables covered in dark-green linen. It was perfect for the theme of the wedding.

At the far end of the room, a bar had been set up. Juanita followed Pedro toward it.

Halfway across the room, Benjy came running up to her. "Nita! Nita! Guess what? Santa came to mah house. Even Mama said so."

"Oh, my! That's wonderful! That makes me so happy." She hugged him.

"Yeah, me too." He grinned at her and ran off.

Juanita turned to greet others in the group. Each in his or her own way was special to the celebration.

She found Maribelle standing with Jake and Ivy.

The woman wore a purple satin dress with a deep décolletage. The color matched the purple in her hair and the hat and netting that framed her sweet, wrinkled face. Her fur stole was wrapped around her shoulders.

"Maribelle, how lovely you look!" Juanita declared, hoping when she reached Maribelle's age, she'd have the panache to handle aging as well as Maribelle.

Smiling with pleasure, Maribelle made a little bow, carefully placing one foot in front of the other. "I knew you'd like it. It was quite the daring thing back in the day. But I've always loved it. So did Henry." She giggled. "And a few others."

Juanita reached for her and hugged her close, careful not to teeter her off balance. She turned to Jake and Ivy. "I see you two have Maribelle in safe hands. I'll stay here for a while. Go off, grab a drink, and enjoy the wonderful appetizers."

Jake turned to Ivy. "We really should test it all. For business." Ivy smiled and accepted his hand as he pulled her into the crowd.

Maribelle smiled. "Those two don't even know the future they have together. But that's something they have to understand on their own."

"Are you tired of standing?" Juanita asked. "Come sit at our table, and I'll get you a plate of appetizers and a glass of champagne."

"Champagne? It's French isn't it? The only real champagne comes from the Champagne region of France around Reims and Epernay. Henry took me there once."

Juanita smiled. "I assure you it's the very best." She loved this woman who had such a colorful past.

As she was helping Maribelle to the table, Pedro came over to them. "Merry Christmas, Maribelle. You look ravishing."

Juanita blinked. *Ravishing? Where had he come up with a word like that?"*

He turned to her and winked. "Been doing a little reading up on our famous friend." He held out his elbow. "Let me escort you, Maribelle. Jake, Ivy, and Benjy are already seated at our table. The others are on their way."

Juanita accompanied them feeling as if she was trailing a member of a royal court. But she didn't mind. She loved that Maribelle was having such a good time.

Once they were seated, drinks were served to everyone, including a special Shirley Temple refreshment for Benjy.

Sitting next to her, Benjy smiled. "Ah lak weddings. Wait raht heah. Ah got somethin' for you and Papa Pedro."

He turned and whispered in Ivy's ear.

She nodded, drew a folded paper from her purse, and handed it to him.

"Heah. For you." Grinning broadly, he handed the paper to her.

Juanita opened it carefully and stared at the drawing of a man and woman. The man had Pedro's mustache and the woman wore her dark hair piled atop her head like her. Standing between the two figures was a boy holding a big, red heart.

"Benjy, thank you. This is beautiful," said Juanita touched to the core.

"It took me a long time to do it," Benjy said proudly, his light-brown eyes shining.

"I have to ask you a question," said Juanita. "In all the other pictures you drew, everyone had a Santa hat. Where are ours?"

He gave her a puzzled look. "You don't need them. Everyone knows you and Papa Pedro are like Christmas all the time."

The few tears Juanita had bravely held back during portions of the wedding ceremony now sprang to her eyes. "Oh, Benjy!" she said, wrapping an arm around him. "You're such a wonderful, wonderful boy."

"Ah know," he said solemnly.

She laughed. "You'd better show this to Papa Pedro."

As Benjy talked to Pedro, Juanita leaned toward Ivy. "Did you see the drawing Benjy made for us?"

Ivy nodded and smiled. "Ah did. He loves the two of you so much." Her cheeks flushed with color. She looked away and back again, and added, "So do Ah."

Aware of what a big admission that was for Ivy to make, Juanita reached over and gave her a warm hug, just as Loretta, Ricardo, and Ken came to the table.

As introductions were made, Maribelle placed a hand on Jake's arm. "Jake is like a son to me. He and Ivy might go into business together one day. Isn't that marvelous?"

At the way Ivy and Jake gazed at one another, Juanita wondered if talk of business was the only thing in their smiles.

Benjy looked up at her. "Mama laks Jake a whole lot."

"How about you?" Juanita asked him.

"Yeah, me too. He makes Mama smile."

Juanita thought back to Pedro's statement about Christmas miracles being good for everybody. It seemed like a lot of them were already taking place.

Amid the sounds of the music from the jazz quartet playing in the corner of the room, dinner was served.

The meal started with a taste of onion soup, followed by a romaine, brie, and walnut salad topped with a balsamic dressing. Filet mignon and salmon choices followed, with all the accompaniments.

As Juanita enjoyed each course, she thought of how her life had changed with her arrival at the Desert Sage Inn so many years ago. Looking around the room, seeing Willow seated beside Craig with the other two Desert Flowers and their spouses, her heart filled with love.

Benjy tugged on her sleeve. "Look! Here comes the cake."

A staff member rolled a cart into the room holding a beautiful, three-tiered wedding cake iced in a lacy white pattern, topped with simple sprigs of mistletoe and holly.

Benjy stared at her wide-eyed. "Did Isaac make that cake?"

Suppressing a smile, Juanita shook her head. "Not this one. Someone here at the hotel did."

"Ah want a big piece," said Benjy, rubbing his stomach.

Ivy leaned over and told him quietly, "We'll all take what we're given."

Benjy nodded, but Juanita noticed he kept his eye on the cake.

After Willow and Craig did the playful taste testing, the cake was served to all. And, later, after all the tables had been cleared, Willow and Craig started off with their dance.

Watching her daughter moving to the music with the man she loved, Juanita thought Willow once more looked like the angel Benjy had called her.

Then it was her and Pedro's turn to exchange partners with them.

After the father and daughter dance and Juanita had taken a spin around the dance floor with Craig, Pedro cut in.

He smiled at her, his eyes lighting as she stepped into his arms.

"You look ravishing tonight," he whispered in her ear.

Ravishing? She chuckled at his attempt to make her feel like Maribelle. "I've never heard you use that word before tonight. And then you said it to Maribelle. Aren't you a little late saying it to me?"

"Never," he said, pulling her closer. "It's never too late to tell my love how beautiful she is. Never."

Feeling Pedro's arms around her, knowing what they'd planned for the future, seeing how happy Willow and Craig were, she filled with happiness as she swayed to the sound of the music. As if from a dreamy distance, she gazed at her friends both old and new and admired the decorations accented with mistletoe and holly.

This day, this very special day, was the best Christmas ever.

# # #

Thank you for reading *The Desert Flowers – Mistletoe and Holly*. If you enjoyed this book, please help other readers discover it by leaving a review on Amazon, BookBub, Goodreads, or your favorite site. It's such a nice thing to do.

Here's a link to where you can sign up for my periodic newsletter: **http://bit.ly/2OQsb7s**

Enjoy an excerpt from my book, *Holiday Hopes*, A Christmas Novella:

CHAPTER ONE

Holly Winters left New York City relieved to have some time at home over the Christmas break, away from the turmoil of teaching English to juniors and seniors in high school. Her mother had made her promise to spend time in Ellenton, New York, with her, claiming it had been way too long since the two of them had had a Hallmark-type holiday together. She'd told Holly that she'd already baked and frozen cookies, had plenty of cocoa in the house, and movies ready to stream on her new television.

Ordinarily, Holly might've rolled her eyes at the suggestion, but it had been one year since her breakup with her boyfriend, and she was ready for "girl" time. She turned on holiday music on her car radio and hummed along. She loved the excitement, the music, the food, and hoped this holiday would be very different from the last when she'd been trying to recover from being dumped.

She'd almost reached the outskirts of Ellenton when her cell rang. She checked caller ID. *Katie Quinn*, her best friend from grammar school to the present day.

"Hey, Katie! What's up?"

"Holly, I'm in desperate need of your help. I've really messed things up this time."

"What now?" Katie always had a crisis of sorts.

"The last admin I placed at Devlin and Sons law firm, just up and quit. I have to find someone right away to replace her. I know you're on your way home, and you wouldn't have to stay at their office long. It's just until I find someone to replace you. Please, pretty please, help me."

"You know I'm here on a break from work, right?" Holly said, sighing.

"Yes, I'm aware of that, but remember when I moved to the city to be with you for an entire week after your breakup with Paul?"

Holly knew she had no choice. "Okay, I'll cover the assignment for you, but you'd better find someone to take my place in a hurry, or you'll have my mother to answer to. This was supposed to be our girl time."

"I'll make it up to both of you somehow," Katie said. "Call me when you get home and are settled. I'll fill you in with the details. And, Holly, I love you."

"Yeah, yeah," said Holly, knowing it was true. They were as close as any friends could be, more like sisters than friends.

Holly pulled into the driveway of the small Cape Cod house where she'd grown up and smiled when her mother rushed out the front door to greet her. They'd always been close, but then, they'd been forced to face the world together after her father unexpectedly died of a heart attack when she was only four.

Holly waved, got out of the car, and eagerly went into her mother's open arms. At fifty-two, Susan Winters was an attractive woman who worked in the maternity ward of the local hospital. The job suited her warm, caring personality.

"Home at last," said her mother. "I'm looking forward to having a few days off with you. I've sent out invitations to my annual Christmas Eve party and expect a nice crowd. Even added a few new people."

Holly cocked an eyebrow at her. "Do you mean young, single men?"

"Just a couple. It's been over a year since you and Paul broke up. It's time to move on." Her mother raised a hand to stop her. "Don't talk to me about being alone. I like it this way."

"Charlie Parker and you have been dating for years. Are you ever going to get married?"

Her mother laughed. "Probably not. At least for a while. We're best of friends, and that's how we like it. But you're young and have always wanted a big family of your own."

"That was before Paul. Now, I'm not sure. Hold on. I'll get my luggage and we can talk inside." Holly went to her car and took out the two suitcases she'd brought with her, glad she'd packed clothes that would be suitable for the temporary job she'd promised to Katie.

Her mother grabbed the handle of one of the suitcases and rolled it up to the front entrance. On either side of the front door, small Alberta spruce trees in pots were decorated with twinkling miniature white lights. A live green wreath with an enormous red bow hung on the door. Inside, Holly knew, a Christmas tree would be waiting for her to decorate with her mother. That was part of the fun of being home for the holidays.

Her mother ushered her inside and to the bedroom in the back of the house that had always been hers.

Holly studied her room, both amused and touched that her mother hadn't changed much about it since she'd left for college ten years ago. The soft-green paint on the walls was inviting and went well with the multi-colored quilt on her cherry, pencil-post bed. The desk she'd studied on in high school still sat in a nook, along with her desk chair. Above the desk was a bulletin board with photographs of various events, including a picture from her college graduation and a photo of Katie and her from high school days.

Seeing it, Holly turned to her mother. "Katie called and asked me for a favor. She needs someone to take over an administrative job at Devlin and Sons law firm, just until she can find a permanent replacement. I couldn't say no after all she did to lift my spirits after Paul and I broke up. I hope you don't mind. We'll still have our evenings together."

Her mother sighed. "I understand, but I hope Katie can find someone quickly. It's a difficult time of the year to be doing that."

Holly put an arm around her mother. "I'm not sure who I'll be working for, but it's all to help her."

"I've heard things haven't been the same there since Duncan Devlin passed. Such a shame. He was much too young to die. Just like your father, he dropped dead of a heart attack."

"I'm sorry. Who's taken his place? His son?"

"That's what I heard. I don't know much about him except he didn't grow up here but lived with his mother somewhere down south."

"Guess that's why I haven't met him," said Holly. "I'd left home by the time he moved here."

"He usually spends time away at the holidays, I understand, which is why he's never come to one of my parties," her mother said. "In fact, after being turned down a couple of times, I haven't sent him an invitation for this year."

"Well, I'll do my duty for Katie and spend the rest of the time with you. I don't want to think of dating or getting involved with anyone here over the holidays. I'm happy with my life in the city."

"How are your little darlings? As cute and smart as always?"

Holly laughed. "It's a good group." Her darlings were rough high school kids who were a joy to teach once you got past the tough role they played. And, yes, some of them were adorable.

"I won't keep you from getting settled any longer," said her mother. "Meet me in the kitchen. I've made some wassail for us to have while decorating the tree."

Holly smiled. She definitely was home for the holidays.

She'd hung the last of her clothes in her closet when her phone rang. *Katie.*

Eager to hear details about the job she'd promised to take, Holly accepted the call.

"Hi, Holly," said Katie. "I've done more investigation into the reason my temp left the law firm and thought it fair that I give you a warning. She was working directly for Corey Devlin, the managing partner of the firm. Apparently, he can be quite demanding. In fact, she told me she was terrified of him. But, Holly, after handling your students, you should have no trouble. He used to be a lot of fun, easier to be around, but since his father died, he's changed. I think things will be fine if you go in there and be yourself."

"Hmmm. He sounds pretty bad, but I'll take care of him," said Holly, sounding more confident than she felt.

"He's going to be away for a couple of days which will give you time to see what the work is like and how you can help. He's left some work for you to do."

Holly paused and then blurted out, "What aren't you telling me? So far he sounds like a donkey."

"I've met him, and I like him. He just needs someone strong to handle him. That's all I'm going to say. You'll figure him out very quickly. And in the meantime, I'll be looking for a replacement."

"Do you want to stop by this evening?" Holly asked.

"Thanks, but I have a date with Evan, but maybe tomorrow." Evan Whicker was the owner of an insurance agency and was a great guy. At one time, Holly had been attracted to him but quickly realized they were not well suited. She was highly organized. He was not. Katie and Evan together were perfect, and Katie was hopeful that Evan was about to give her an engagement ring.

"Ready to come trim the tree?" her mother asked, handing her a cup of the hot, cinnamon spicy liquid—her own recipe for old-fashioned wassail.

Holly took a sip and let out a soft murmur of delight. On this crisp, cold afternoon, it tasted delicious. She took off her boots and slipped into the fuzzy slippers she left in Ellenton for use and padded to the living room.

She glanced at the tall, round tree and inhaled the evergreen scent that emanated from it. "Smells good," she said. "Did Charlie put it up for you?"

Her mother smiled. "As always, the darling."

"Is he coming here tonight?" Holly asked. She thought Charlie was perfect for her mother and couldn't understand why they didn't get married. But each time she broached the subject, her mother shut her down.

"No, he's not. This is our time together. I've invited him for dinner tomorrow, though. He was almost as anxious to see you as I."

Holly looked at the neat cardboard boxes stacked on the floor. "Should we get started?"

Her mother raised her mug. "Yes! Here's to a wonderful holiday season. It's such a joy to be able to share it with you."

"Hear! Hear!" said Holly, gently clinking her mug against

her mother's.

They set down their mugs and opened one of the boxes. Ornaments of all kinds were nestled inside. Her mother had collected special glass ornaments for years, and Holly felt like she was opening a gift each time she lifted one from the box.

Both Holly and her mother were fussy about displaying each ornament properly. They'd only finished one of the two boxes when the oven timer sounded.

"You go ahead and work on it. I'll check the casserole and put the rest of the dinner together," said her mother.

Holly nodded, lifted a little elf ornament, and hung it from a perfect branch up high in the tree. Satisfied with the way it looked, she stepped away and headed into the kitchen. She knew what her mother was having for dinner even before she smelled it.

A lemon chicken casserole was one of her favorites. That and a crisp, green lettuce salad was the perfect way to start off the visit.

Inside the kitchen, her mother served the casserole while Holly tossed the lettuce with a balsamic dressing.

Sitting at the table across from her mother, a sudden sting of tears startled Holly. Even though her family was small, she was happy to be home at the holidays and felt sorry for those who were alone at such a time.

Later, after the last ornament had been hung and the boxes put away, her mother announced she was going to bed.

Holly was happy to do the same. It had been a rough, few weeks at school, and she was ready to relax and rest. Then she remembered her commitment to Katie. She'd have to set the alarm clock because she couldn't be late to her new job.

# # #

About the Author

Judith Keim, a *USA Today* Best-Selling Author, is a hybrid author who both has a publisher and self-publishes, Ms. Keim writes heart-warming novels about women who face unexpected challenges, meet them with strength, and find love and happiness along the way. Her best-selling books are based, in part, on many of the places she's lived or visited, and on the interesting people she's met, creating believable characters and realistic settings her many loyal readers love. Ms. Keim loves to hear from her readers and appreciates their enthusiasm for her stories.

Ms. Keim enjoyed her childhood and young-adult years in Elmira, New York, and now makes her home in Boise, Idaho, with her husband and their two dachshunds, Winston and Wally, and other members of her family.

While growing up, she was drawn to the idea of writing stories from a young age. Books were always present, being read, ready to go back to the library, or about to be discovered. All in her family shared information from the books in general conversation, giving them a wealth of knowledge and vivid imaginations.

"I hope you've enjoyed this book. If you have, please help other readers discover it by leaving a review on Amazon, BookBub, Goodreads, or the site of your choice. And please check out my other books and series:

Hartwell Women Series
The Beach House Hotel Series
The Fat Fridays Group
The Salty Key Inn Series
The Chandler Hill Inn Series
Seashell Cottage Books
The Desert Sage Inn Series
Soul Sisters at Cedar Mountain Lodge
The Sanderling Cove Inn Series
The Lilac Lake Inn Series

ALL THE BOOKS ARE NOW AVAILABLE IN AUDIO on, Audible, iTunes, Findaway, Kobo, Google, and other sites! So fun to have these characters come alive!"

Ms. Keim can be reached at **www.judithkeim.com**

And to like her author page on Facebook and keep up with the news, go to: **http://bit.ly/2pZWDgA**

To receive notices about new books, follow her on Book Bub:
https://www.bookbub.com/authors/judith-keim

And here's a link to where you can sign up for her periodic newsletter: **http://bit.ly/2OQsb7s**

She is also on Twitter @judithkeim, LinkedIn, and Goodreads. Come say hello!

Acknowledgments

Thank you to the staff of the Historical Society and Museum of Palm Desert for taking the time to talk to us and make the history of the area come alive. And, as always, I am eternally grateful to my team of editors, Peter Keim and Lynn Mapp, my book cover designer, Lou Harper, and my narrator for Audible and iTunes, Angela Dawe. They are the people who take what I've written and help turn it into the book I proudly present to you, my readers! I also wish to thank my coffee group of writers who listen and encourage me to keep on going. Thank you, Peggy, Lynn, Cate, Nikki Jean, and Megan. And to you, my fabulous readers, I thank you for your continued support and encouragement. Without you, this book would not be present.